MW00586342

ALSO BY CHUCK PALAHNIUK

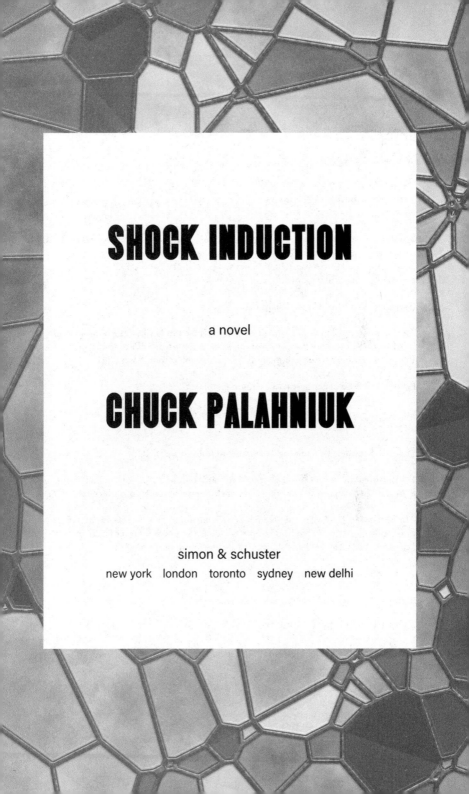

SHOCK INDUCTION

a novel

CHUCK PALAHNIUK

simon & schuster

new york   london   toronto   sydney   new delhi

SIMON & SCHUSTER

1230 Avenue of the Americas
New York, NY 10020

First Simon & Schuster hardcover edition October 2024

SIMON & SCHUSTER and colophon are registered trademarks of Simon & Schuster, LLC

Simon & Schuster: Celebrating 100 Years of Publishing in 2024

For information about special discounts for bulk purchases, please contact Simon & Schuster Special Sales at 1-866-506-1949 or business@simonandschuster.com.

The Simon & Schuster Speakers Bureau can bring authors to your live event. For more information or to book an event, contact the Simon & Schuster Speakers Bureau at 1-866-248-3049 or visit our website at www.simonspeakers.com.

Interior design by Carly Loman

Manufactured in the United States of America

10 9 8 7 6 5 4 3 2 1

Library of Congress Cataloging-in-Publication Data is available.

ISBN 978-1-6680-2144-6
ISBN 978-1-6680-2146-0 (ebook)

SHOCK INDUCTION

WARNING: Do not touch your eyes or mouth while reading this book. To lessen the risk of acute ERE poisoning, take frequent breaks to wash your hands for the duration of the story. To protect your health, wash your hands thoroughly, using soap and warm water.

1

Want to control other people? One method of induction depends on exhausting the subject's mind. Ply the subject with so many details they lose the ability to focus on any single one.

Tire them until their eyes glaze over.

If you must, picture a person. A person not so young they bank on every haircut being a fresh start. A person old enough to recall when the top of all windshields was colored blue. Can you picture that? Every day, a blue sky. Such optimism.

Let's start with that much.

Now give yourself a big hug. You're doing great!

Adjusting for variables in household income in recent recorded history circa 2032, the United States Senate Subcommittee on Education sat down with industry leaders from strategy-based commercial publishing for the stated purpose of identifying and ameliorating the environmental factors perpetuating the persistent and substantial gap of no less than two standard deviations in educational outcomes evident between grouped gender and ethnic cohorts specific to urban-sensitive populations.

Factoring in raw data, not limited to corollary subsets, sourced from sixteen distinct cohorts and adjusted, plus or minus two percent, for overall physical and emotional well-being as well as socioeconomic-status inequities and the implementable strictures of realistic policy response, given how the variable figure is an artifact of both performative and empirical significance at least as measurable quantifiable skills attainment

might diverge, those present engaged with the quandary as to reasons academic learners had so recently failed to engage with long-form prose.

Allowing for the first and last quintile, the resultant cognitive mean skills gap, provable by intersectional juxtaposition and by forgoing traits non-applicable to increased resource investment in pre-K through post-secondary settings.

In abstract they asked: Why the heck isn't anyone reading *Moby-Dick?*

Are you tired yet?

Another method to induce a hypnotic trance is fractionation.

You call the subject's attention in different directions. Listen to the sounds around you. Listen. Focus on the smooth feel of the paper under your fingertips, focus on the brush and peel as you turn the next page.

Picture a girl. Picture Samantha Deel. If you must, picture Samantha's uncle. Samantha Deel has an uncle who served the better part of a seven-year sentence in prison. This uncle registers as a sex offender.

Although he's wheelchair bound, Sam's uncle still reports to his parole officer every week, all because he one time "forgot" a safe word during sex. Most of his adult life, Sam's uncle spends every waking moment grumbling to himself, "Avocado. Avo-

cado. Avocado. Avocado. Avocado. Avocado. Avocado. *Avocado.* Avocado. Avocado. Avocado. Avocado. Avocado. Avocado. Avocado. Avocado. Avocado. Avocado. Avocado. Avocado. Avocado. Avocado. Avocado. Avocado. Avocado. Avocado. Avocado. Avo-cado. *Avocado.* Avocado. Avocado. Avocado. Avocado. Avocado. Avocado. Avocado. Avocado. Avocado. Avocado. Avocado. Avo-cado. Avocado. Avocado. Avocado. Avocado. Avocado. Avocado. Avocado. Avocado. Avocado. Avocado. Avocado. Avocado. Avo-cado. Avocado. Avocado. Avocado."

Picture Samantha's mother, a woman who once complained about the court-ordered Intoxalock device on her car. "I don't have to drink," Sam's mom said. "Even if I've just been eating a Cinnabon or huffing gasoline, it can still blow a false positive."

Picture Samantha's father, who once carried his Weatherby SA-08 twenty-gauge into the woods. Between racoon season and upland quail, he walked out to shoot mistletoe from the crown of a white oak. A big dark mass of mistletoe, if you can picture it, a month's rent hiding high up among the oak branches. Samantha's father shouldered the rifle and squinted down the barrel at the dark shape in the leaves. He braced with one foot back and pulled the trigger, Sam's father did, and that great clump of mistletoe came crashing down. Except it wasn't mistletoe.

A body fell at his feet, Mr. Deel had killed a man. Except the man was already dead, with a noose of rope knotted around his neck, the skin as thin as a coat of paint on the dead man's bones. A suicide, her father had shot down.

Except the dead man spoke. He lay at the feet of Samantha's dad, busted from the falling impact, from battering so many sturdy oak branches, this man, the noose still cinched around his neck and the rope blasted in half.

Listen, and you can hear the half-dead man peppered with buckshot, bleeding from the holes in his clothes but still mutter-ing to himself, "Avocado. Avocado. Avocado. Avocado. Avocado. Avocado. Avocado. Avocado. *Avocado . . .*"

3

Feel the heft of the book in your hands.
That's fractionation induction.

The anecdote also demonstrates cognitive reframing.
Spin = Cognitive Reframing.

Please think of this first part as the opposite of a wake-up call.
Wonderful. You're doing just great. You're doing great.
Big hug.

If you've read this far you've already read too far. Go wash your hands.

The Senate findings committee had fingered gaming and online pornography as the primary driving factors for the outcome of functional illiteracy.

"Gaming and movies are nothing but light and sound," the Senate stated. They asked, "What do we have to throw at them?"

An editor from big publishing hovered over the microphone. "Senator, in 2032 alone, more than twelve hundred people died from handling dollar bills laced with fentanyl." For effect, here the editor hesitated. "I submit for your approval a glorious new future for books and the readers who love them. May I present the ERE Program."

***Excerpted with full permission from* Regular Ward Care for Comatose ERE Patients**

In cases of acute ERE poisoning, withhold tracheal intubation. At all times, pay close attention to respiration. Always note when bronchial encumbrance in the comatose patient requires the use of airway clearance

techniques (ACTs). Be aware of end-stage wet respirations, also known as the "death rattle" . . .

In that closed-door secret subcommittee meeting in the Department of Education, the editor finally asked, "Can you see where this is headed?"

2

Of Sam's childhood, one memory stands out with crystal clarity. A winter night. A bitter ice storm had left her family with no water. The cold had frozen the pipes of their cramped apartment. Her mother and father and crippled uncle sat in the icy kitchenette swilling NyQuil straight from the bottle. Sunken into themselves with self-loathing.

As little Samantha cowered at their feet, hungry for love and acknowledgment, the lights went out. The room was plunged into darkness.

At that, her father looked up with confused eyes, and with green-stained lips said, "Sammy, the wires have frozen, too!"

In the longer, longer version: Sam: Sam the Magnificent: Samantha Deel. What's important is you love Sam before you hate Sam.

Visual induction.

To this day, Sam's church says No Open Doors. No matter how hot the morning, the front doors, you can't prop them open. Only no one ever says how come.

Big hug.

Samantha is how come.

Not that she held a grudge against Jesus. But this is the ending you should always circle back around to. To Esmond Jensen's funeral, when someone broke that rule.

The church where the Deels used to go, they're saving up for air-conditioning. And a new window. Before you throw in all the burning candles and the incense smoke, a billboard-big stained-

glass window used to shine in above the altar. The place was an oven.

Used to be an oven.

A colored-glass Jesus descending from Heaven on glowing clouds, that window, crowded around by pink angel babies. Jesus floating up there above a world of stained-glass flowers in colors that scar your retina. Colors like a welding arc or the center of a burning road flare. The sunlight threw a rainbow shadow over the Deel family and wheelchair-bound uncle. It turned everyone radioactive blues and fireworks yellow.

High up as she was in the choral loft, Samantha sweated in her choir robe. The church organ blasted the hot air through its pipes. Sam stepped forward from the ranks, ready to begin her solo, when a phrase sprang to mind: "This furnace of music . . ." A phrase from *The Hunchback of Notre-Dame.* The story of a deaf bell ringer. Per Victor Hugo, ". . . the bells had broken the drums of his ears; he had become deaf."

As Samantha Deel waited to sing the first notes of her special, she looked over the mourners who stood below the gallery. Black veiled and hatted. As she awaited her cue, Sam searched her mind for the names the hunchback had given his bells. Jacqueline, for one. Marie, another. Thibauld and Guillaume and Gabrielle.

In the book, the hunchback of Notre-Dame had rallied his bells like a football coach would his players. "Go on," said the hunchback, "go on, go on, Gabrielle, pour out all thy noise into the Place, 'tis a festival to-day. No laziness, Thibauld; thou art relaxing; go on, go on, then, art thou rusted, thou sluggard? That is well! Quick! Quick! Let not thy clapper be seen! Make them all deaf like me!"

On the occasion of Esmond Jensen's funeral. His being laid to rest. On that last day anybody ever propped open the front door, the breeze brought in something sparkling green.

Some tiny fairy buzzed up the center aisle, drawn in by flow-

ered hats. Attracted by the urns that flank the altar. Urns full-to-toppling with orange gladiolas. Pink gladiolas.

Full-throated singing now, Sam's sparkling bundle of strette, trills, and arpeggios, they falter. She's been upstaged. Some green spark buzzed through the haze of pipe-organ music and incense. It unrolled a thin tongue to drink at the gladiolas. A delight, this flash of emerald green wings, it tried to drink at the plaster lilies in the arms of the Virgin Mary statue. It darted between gladiolas and potted chrysanthemums, upstaging Father Caswell and the altar boys.

No one heard the eulogy. They're all finger pointing. Whisper shouting. Eyes pinned on this bright little angel.

A voice, clear and shrill with delight, said, "A hummingbird!" And the shining miracle had a name. It jetted between the window of St. Agatha of Sicily getting her breasts cut off by Roman soldiers and the window of St. Lawrence burning naked on a giant barbeque. It soared higher, looking for a way out through the stained-glass Heavens.

The choir stopped singing. The pipe organ stopped. Parishioners ducked as the green light rocketed and dove above their heads.

Tiny as a piece of jewelry, it settled on the plaster halo of St. Patrick. Its beak hung open, panting. Its tiny heartbeat seeable under slippery, green feathers.

Samantha slipped down from the choir loft into the aisle. Her church shoes, called Mary Janes. Black patent leather with a buckle strap across the top part and a stubby heel, called a kitten heel. The training bra for a girl's feet before real high heels.

Samantha, in her pleated choir robe, she crept up the aisle toward the altar where the bird waited. Crept past Esmond Jensen's closed casket.

The bird launched itself at other flowers, the glass daffodils in the window, below the feet of Christ. That one hungry hummingbird pecked at the blazing-hot yellow lilies. Licked its pointed

tongue against blistering red roses. Up there, ceiling-high, a blast furnace that high. It bashed itself against the glowing everything of that wall of sunlight.

This blur and buzz was beating itself to death against what it couldn't understand. Flowers without nectar.

Seen up close, stained glass amounts to a huge jigsaw puzzle. That great tonnage of glass, jigsawed together and bound at the seams by soft strands of lead. Lead strips soldered at the joints to make a wall-sized network of black metal. A towering wall as thin as cardboard, but as heavy as stone.

Samantha crept up to where the hummingbird was battering itself into a heart attack. She slipped off one shoe and swung the heel to smash a glass tulip. Ruby slivers went everywhere and the vandalism sound. Air and light poured in through the new hole, only the smash drove the little bird higher. To where Samantha had to climb onto the windowsill to hammer her heel to bash out a glass nasturtium.

Samantha Deel hammered out glass peonies and baby glass lambs and chunks of sky, leaving jagged holes lined with a few colored glass teeth. Before Father Caswell could stop her, she left big sections of the window nothing but the network of metal strips that had bound the glass together. The webbing of thin lead outlines that had divided flowers from sky from baby lambs.

And as the hummingbird panicked and flew higher, Sam climbed.

Back then, way back when, Samantha Deel could still hear people shouting at her, but she continued to climb. Only faster. Before gravity or hands could pull her back to the ground, on that ropey ladder of lead strips, that lace of soft metal. Like a lead spider's web just strong enough to support the weight of one high schooler. Anyone else, any extra weight would pull the whole stained-glass Heavens down around their heads.

The hands of Sam's mom and dad reached up to drag their child back or break her fall.

Sam's mom and dad shouted, "Samantha!" Shouted, "Miss Girlie-girl!" Trying to call her back down to Earth. Dodging not to catch a sliver of Christ in the eye.

Sam climbed that soft, sagging network of lead. Like a pirate climbing the rigging of a ship. Always swinging her shoe to bust out another escape hatch. Always scaring the bird to fly higher among the scorching-hot angels. Her fingerprints sliced to mush, she climbed into the masterpiece clouds and perfect rays of fake sunshine and shoe-smashed an angel's lovely face so the hummingbird might live.

Samantha busted out the brocade robes and jeweled crowns, and her bloody hands found new grips where the fake blood of the Christ's hands had been. Her bloody feet found toeholds where the fake blood of His feet had been.

And the fresh air gushed in. A breeze that blew out all their candles.

And the hummingbird was always higher, too high to save. Too scared for Sammy to rescue.

Her legs dangled from the pleated skirt of her choir robe; her legs streaked with blood. And looking up, Father Caswell saw flowers. Flowered panties. Making everyone look elsewhere.

The shattered pink and gold of sandals and halos sprayed down so no one saw how the sagging spiderweb was already giving way when Sam the Magnificent hauled back her arm. With one mighty swing she nailed Jesus Christ in His beautiful glass face. Busted not just His nose and glass jaw but His everything with the heel of her Mary Jane.

Apologies to George Orwell.

Apologies to everyone except God who knows a picture isn't God, it doesn't matter how pretty.

But through where Jesus had been there was real blue sky and the hummingbird escaped back to real everything to live another day. Breaking and exiting. For better or worse.

Now instead of being stained vivid blues and sulfur yellows,

minus the stained-glass shadow, Samantha's mom and dad turned back to their regular color.

All the church's hot air began to leak out that God-shaped hole.

All that's left up above is the glass parts still intact. The glass sun shining through the glass clouds, hanging high up, waiting to come down guillotine style.

The bird escaped even as the buckling, sagging, stretched-out framework of Heaven began to slowly, slowly, ever so slowly deliver Samantha Deel into the hands of an angry mob.

This is the part hypnotists call *The Buy-In.*

That was visual induction.

Another method for controlling people? Hypnotists call it *guided meditation.*

You walk up to a gate. Against your hand, the iron of the gate feels cold.

You push the gate open. The rusted hinges give a creak. You hear gravel crunch as you step forward onto a path. A hummingbird cuts and buzzes, buzzes and zigzags, pulling your attention to roses. White roses.

You smell white roses, and the hummingbird hopscotches, jets, dive-bombs to draw your attention to a heavy, hanging curtain. Ruby-throated, emerald-crested, the hummingbird hums up to a clothesline sagging with damp wedding gowns hung out to dry. But more wedding dresses than you've ever seen together. Floor length. Skirt-heavy, pleated and flared wedding gowns.

The hummingbird disappears up the skirts. Ivory-colored, eggshell-colored wedding gowns. Not gowns at all, but flowers. A

gallows of flowers, fleshy as orchids. The clothesline turns out to be a bush blossoming with flowers.

You smell vanilla, vanilla edging to suntan oil bordering on baby powder sparking to cedar-chest sweaters folded with layers of tissue paper, that smell you smell.

The bell-shaped flowers hang there. *Brugmansia arborea.*

Repeat to yourself: Ketamine. Adderall. Ritalin. Shazam. Sodium chlorate. Doxepin. Flurazepam. Alakazam. Quazepam. Quasimodo. Words like a magician might say.

Another thing to keep in mind is lucid dreaming.

Picture the Deel household, if you must. Picture a place where joy comes one morning when you stand up and find the toilet bowl filled with blood. The clump of toilet tissue you hold is blotted with blood. Despite all your best efforts, death makes itself known. No more Christmas. No more dreams of retirement and travel to Paris. Death shows up in the bathroom. Game over.

But then it hits you, the joy does. You ate a beet salad yesterday. The blood running down your leg isn't blood.

3

After the church ordeal, Mr. Deel said no more singing. At home, after church, he said, "Not in my house, no lessons! Not on my dime!" After she'd been bandaged up at the emergency room.

Samantha said, "But my voice is my ticket out of here!"

Her father shook his head. "We're not wasting any more of our hardened [*sic*] money on your pipe dream!"

At home in the shadow of trophies, trophies for choir, trophies for Best Vocalist, Momma Deel said, "Then *after college!*" She said, "We're not paying for you to waste your life!"

Samantha said, "You can't just pull the plug!" She looked at the floor. Looked up. She said the unsayable. "Dad, just this once, look at me." She waited until his eyes met hers. "I'm fat, all right?"

Both her parents winced. Her mom started to say a word, but it never came out.

Sam continued, "I'm never going to be pretty, not like Mom." She pitched the words a little lower. "But my voice is my ticket out of here."

Samantha blinked back tears. "I'm never going to be smart like you. I'm fat and ugly, but I have this one gift."

Then she said the other unsayable. "People get law degrees and still end up broke."

Her mom tossed back an emergency-room Percodan and said, "Broke is not an option." Her mom worked a corkscrew into the soft cardboard of a wine box.

Sam fumbled to help. "It doesn't do like that, Mom."

Her mom balked. The box tore to reveal the bag of wine within, the bag snagged and pinot blanc began trickling from the leak.

Then Sam held up her bandaged hands and said the other unsayable. "People get law degrees and still kill themselves."

And here Momma Deel went in for a hug and said, "If it's a mission in life you want? You can go rinse out your uncle's diapers in the bathtub." She said, "And don't be too squeamish to push the crap down the drain with your fingers."

Sam's father tipped a shot of vodka into the prescription bottle of Percodans. As the pills dissolved, he tipped the bottle to his lips and drank. He wiped the white sludge from his mouth and said, "If you're going to throw away your life . . ." He took a second sip. "You might as well marry the king of Finland."

From his wheelchair, Sam's uncle said, "Avocado. Avocado. Avocado. Avocado. Avocado. Avocado. Avocado. Avocado. Avocado. Avocado. Avocado. Avocado. Avocado. Avocado. Avocado."

Here Sam hit Ctrl+Alt+Breaking&Exiting. To plan her escape.

In the longer version, still, Anne Lewis-Kennedy died by her own hand. Anne, the goer of the extra mile. Toer of lines.

To pile detail upon detail. To tire you out.

Anne Lewis-Kennedy, the walker of the straight and narrow, and all-'round early birder. A memorizer of the Periodic Table, she'd piled the Lewis-Kennedy bathtub full of dry ice and locked the bathroom door and stretched out on the terry-cloth bath mat, knowing carbon dioxide is heavier than air. That dry ice is frozen CO_2, and that as it melts it releases that colorless gas. Almost odorless, a little sour and sharp, carbon dioxide is the smell of soda pop if you subtracted the sugar.

This carbon dioxide is what humane slaughterhouses use. Pigs and chickens breathe it, and within twelve seconds they pass out.

Within twelve clock ticks Anne Lewis-Kennedy had felt giddy,

a giggling feeling, and most likely she'd seen rainbow visions just before she'd fallen asleep. Within a few minutes, she'd suffocated.

Your eyelids feel heavy. Your arms feel limp and heavy.

Picture a newspaper headline:

Revere Consolidated High School: "Suicide High."

As the subcommittee watched, the editor lifted a briefcase and set it on the table, and opened the briefcase and lifted something out. The editor held this object, brown-colored, square, high above everyone's head and asked, "Esteemed Senators, how many of you have read . . ."

The editor looked at the object, at its cover, at words printed on the cover, and asked, *"Moby-Dick?"*

Up in her bedroom Sam had scattered bottles of pills all over the bed. Sitting cross-legged on her bedspread, leaned back against a bank of stuffed animals. Stuffed elephants' and bears' little bodies. Little pill bottles. Orange pills. Sam's hands twist off child-guard caps. Pluck out cotton balls. Chuck the cotton to the floor. Pouring the pills into an orange pile on the bedspread beside her leg.

She asks, "Do you know what geniuses have in common." Her mouth, already stained orange. Her scarred fingertips, her fingerprints erased by scars from stained glass. Orange stained her fingertips, too.

With orange lips she drops the names Thomas Edison, Ludwig Beethoven, Howard Hughes. Her orange teeth crunch pills into orange spit.

With one hand she holds a bottle of water, the screw top

stained orange from her mouth. With her other hand, she plucks pills from the pile and puts them between her lips. A steady *crunch-crunch* comes from between her back teeth.

Sam asks, "Do you remember who Shelley Beattie was? The American Gladiators, on television, she was the one named Siren." That constant *crunch-crunch.*

Between sips of water, she name-drops David Hockney and Francisco Goya.

Sam's set her turntable and collection of vinyl against one wall alongside all of her choral sheet music. Hung on the wall is something framed, under glass. A blue eye. Part of the Jesus face she'd busted out to save the hummingbird. Glass under glass.

The Jesus eye hangs there. Watching.

Aspirin after aspirin gets *crunch-crunch*ed.

Shelley Beattie had been the hero to millions of kids. The American Gladiator from television. She'd killed herself in 2008. "But that's not why she was a hero," Sam adds. She sips from the water bottle. Swallows orange gunk. An orange backwash turns the water in the bottle orange.

Aspirin, she says. Acetaminophen, she says. It was first derived from white willow bark when Aristotle used it to treat pain. An overdose, she says, will bring on salicylism.

Still, her chopped-up hand picks orange pills from the pill pile and takes them to her mouth.

At the age of three Shelley Beattie had eaten an overdose because it tasted like candy. Salicylism blocks blood flow to the inner ear. It depletes the protein glutathione, Sam explains. The cochlea dies.

"It's called the *cochlea*," Sam says, "because it looks like a sea shell."

When you put a shell to your ear, you hear the ocean due to a shell inside your ear. A pretty balance. But after salicylism, your inner ear dies, and you end up like the famous talk-radio guy and the movie star who went deaf from Vicodin.

"It's the same dynamic," Sam the Magnificent explains. The sea shell inside your ear, it dies.

Thomas Edison, Howard Hughes, Francisco Goya, they'd accomplished great works because they could concentrate. They weren't distracted from their visions, because they couldn't hear. They were deaf. Shelley Beattie, aka Siren, had been the hero to millions of deaf children.

Rush Limbaugh and Melanie Griffith.

Sam asks, "Can you see where I'm going with this?"

Since 1960-something baby aspirin has come in little bottles because so many children have overdosed on it. Critics call it *candy aspirin.* Child-guard caps were invented to stem a rising flood of deaf toddlers.

If the world won't listen to Sam singing, then she refuses to listen to the world. She wants to spend the rest of her life in a David Hockney, Hellen Keller, Beethoven bubble of silence. Wherever she walks she will have room in her own brain to work.

Her back teeth *crunch-crunch* on the pills. The pile on her bed shrinks. Sam the Magnificent will go into a self-exile. Like Thoreau. Like Bernard Shaw fleeing to Ireland to write. Orwell, down and out in London and Paris. Anymore, it's almost impossible to find the isolation needed to develop a unique voice, she explains.

If she can't sing, Sam doesn't want her ears.

After that day, Sam's world looked faked. A performance. A silent world wherein other people seemed to lip-synch to nothing. And when Sam failed to hear them, their silly facial expressions only grew bigger and sillier. Their hands flew around, and their mouths stretched bigger while the cords in their necks stood out in sharp relief.

Everyone became a terrible mime.

For now, give yourself another big hug. You're doing great!

One time, Momma Deel stood in front of a mirror. Momma Deel held a glass of wine in one hand and wore only a nylon slip. As her eyes traced the bulges and the sags in the mirror, Momma Deel said, "I'm like an oak tree." She lifted the glass to her lips and took a sip of wine. "You could cut me in half and count the stretch marks."

Then Garson Stavros took his own life. Garson, the head of Science Club and a fanatic for everything STEM. Junior varsity center and sinker of a thousand foul shots, a first-round draft pick with a full-ride scholarship to Tulane.

Garson, who had everything to live for. Another fan of carbon dioxide, or a possible copycat, Garson had volunteered to work the closing shift at the Dairy Freez. To mop up. Alone in the fast-food kitchen he'd unhooked the CO_2 canisters from the soda lines and dragged both canisters into the walk-in freezer. He'd worn his coat over his uniform as he'd unscrewed the hissing valves on each canister and closed the freezer door. First giddy. Then giggling. Then asleep and dead within twelve clock ticks. Another death chalked up to carbon dioxide.

Since these weren't the mouth-breather kids, the losers and knuckle draggers, the newspaper ran the headline *Honor Society Suicides.*

By then the school district was calling it a cluster.

4

Dirty talk can be its own form of hypnotic induction.

"You like my big dick, don't you? You love getting stuffed by Daddy's fat piece of meat. Tell me how much you love this fat cock, Stephany. Squeal for me."

Squeal.

Another method of induction is to create a pattern, then to repeat the pattern. Then to vary the pattern. Then to break the pattern. All the while, your subject will hang on. Hungry for repetition.

You can spend your whole life waiting for the pattern to repeat.

Jay Gatsby did.

Addressing the esteemed Senate Subcommittee on Education, the editor said, "You know, when you're playing fetch with your dog?" The editor paused for effect. "You know how sometimes you only *pretend to throw the ball*?" The editor waited for the image to set in. "And your dog runs off sniffing?"

The editor waited for a laugh to build.

As the editor put it before the Senate Subcommittee on Education, "Esteemed colleagues, why are books banned in so many legal detention facilities?" The editor paused for a response.

None came. "In a locked-down world of incarceration, why do we continue to deny prisoners ready access to copies of *Moby-Dick*?"

Hovering over the microphone, the editor asked, "Senators, why do we actively, each year, prevent thousands of *Little Women*s [*sic*] from reaching prisoners on every level of our incarceration system!" The editor looked from Senator to Senator. "Every year! Every year, our law-enforcement agents burn more copies of *To Kill a Mockingbird* and *Catcher in the Rye* . . ."

The editor glanced down to the notes laid out on the table. "Why do we destroy millions of books every year?"

The editor continued. "And we don't simply shred the books. We burn them. In fact, our government currently burns more copies of *Moby-Dick* and *Jane Eyre* than the German Nazi brownshirts ever dreamed of burning during Hitler's reign."

Why is that?

Enter the achievement gap of 2032, an all-time gulf between the haves and the have-nots.

The qualifiable proof that reading skills had dropped to the point that most post-secondary students were functionally illiterate. Proof that modern education had failed students.

Black and white. Male and female. No one was reading at grade level.

Samantha pinches her thumb and index finger together and makes them peck at the palm of her other hand. *Chicken* in American Sign Language. She pulls an invisible turd from one elbow. Sam smacks the tip of her index finger against her own chin. *Bitch.*

Her hands could now say *Chicken-shit bitch.*

"The Achilles tendon of gaming and online pornography," said the editor, addressing the Senate Subcommittee on Closing the Achievement Gap in Education, "is that games and porno force the user to do all of the work."

And with that, the editor proposed a fix for everything.

Submitted here for your consideration: The funeral for Garson Stavros. The kid who chose suicide over a full-ride basketball scholarship to Tulane.

Today they've put Garson inside a heavy wooden box. Polished ebony with brass handles, a box any magician would be proud to use onstage. They've laid Garson Stavros out straight and shut the lid. Latched and locked it tight. Air tight. Organ music plays.

They've placed the box in front of the altar, with Father Caswell standing by. The stained-glass window still not replaced, just patched over with plywood.

At the foot of the plywood window stands a box marked for donations toward new stained glass.

Samantha Deel's blood still stains the carpet if you know where to look.

Locked in that box, Stavros might have a few inhales' worth of air to breathe.

Breathe in as much air as you can. Hold your breath.

Watching now, Sam isn't scared. Her boyfriend was an escape artist.

No one else appears to worry. Witness Mrs. Stavros standing there, looking anywhere except at the box with her son locked inside. Just look at Mr. Stavros, too, twiddling a cigarette, unlit, between the fingers of one hand. Mr. Stavros shrugs and says, "I guess I picked the wrong time to give up smoking!"

His wife pops out a little laugh. The corners of her mouth tuck up into little pockets that read as happy.

Their son is locked inside an air-tight box. No telling how long

he's been inside. He's been locked in there since before anyone else had arrived. Half of the high school stands around. We're talking as many people as a town. The sophomore class has sent a bunch of flowers, a big wreath of carnations in red and gold, the team colors of the Battling Beefeaters. The varsity cheerleaders stand beside the box, all long legs, all big hair, like a team of magic assistants looking sad.

Near the coffin, picture a young man standing. If you will, a young man, a stranger so far. A man not so old he wouldn't beat the snot out of you, he stands with both hands balled into fists. Jackbooted. Neck tattooed. A kid named War Dog, with eyes sunk so close together they could be touching behind the bridge of his nose, War Dog. He holds his entire body in a fist. A recent transfer student to Suicide High.

5

Under your breath, say, "Presto-change-o." Say, "Flurazepam."

The trick is to hijack the rational mind. Distract critical thinking so that you engage the subconscious.

At the funeral, a perfume smell steps closer. Two manicured hands say, "Greetings, Miss Deel." This is Mrs. Terry from fourth period. From Statistics class. In black she looks like a witch, her dress black. Inky immaculate. Black shoes with pointed toes. The strap of a black purse is looped over one arm. She looks at Samantha and her lips say, "I guess you'll be our valedictorian next year." She signs, "Have they found the dog, yet?"

Garson Stavros's dog, she means, half Jack Russell, half everything else. A dog between purse-sized and Marmaduke. Garson's mom had named the dog Paisley.

Sam shakes her head, No.

Mrs. Terry's lips continue, "Paisley ran away." From her purse she lifts her phone. On the screen, Mrs. Terry pulls up a photo of Garson Stavros hugging the dog.

Someone, a man, to judge from the sound of it, blows his nose. Another guidance counselor or coach.

Samantha's hands sign the words, "Open sesame."

Nodding like she knows a secret, like the witch she might be, Mrs. Terry's lips say, "Someone ought to go out. A smart person should walk around and rescue that poor dog." She winks.

War Dog watches the coffin.

War Dog watches Samantha.

Samantha is watching them bury her boyfriend.

"Senators, bear witness," the editor said, and held aloft a book. A plain hardcover book. "I hold in my hand," said the editor, "a new 'Enhanced Reader' edition of *Moby-Dick* guaranteed to sell more than fifty, nay, more than *one hundred million* copies."

The room gasped.

A *For Sale* sign stands at the foot of the Stavroses' driveway. A *Sold* sticker already plastered across the *Sale Pending* part. A black wreath still hangs on the front door. Profits from the sale of the house were going to the Knights of Columbus.

Someone has left casserole dishes on the front doorstep. A lot of people, from the look of it. Bowls of potato salad sweat under plastic wrap. Black flies hover over it all.

Samantha stoops to place a bouquet of flowers against the door, in a makeshift memorial, where the dying stubs of candles flicker black smoke.

Heaped around the base of the real-estate agent's sign, a stack of cardboard boxes offer left-behind stuff. The night's dew has soaked the cardboard. Some corners have split to spill out a basketball uniform. Nikes. Larger boxes have split across the word *FREE* written in black marker on the sides.

Littered around the left-behind books and trophies are plastic bones riddled with teeth marks. Loose fur covers a discarded dog bed. Sam leans down and takes a rubber toy molded to look like a bright red T-bone steak. Sam squeezes the steak and it gives out a loud squeal.

Across the street, a curtain parts. A face appears in a window. A woman in a bathrobe holds a cup of coffee, she hovers there and disappears.

Sam squeaks the T-bone steak and her hands call out, "Paisley!" She signs louder, "Paisley!" The squeak sounds thin and

shrill in the chilly air. Elsewhere, a dog jumps behind a fence. Another dog jumps inside a window. Neither are Paisley.

Among the books lies one with a peanut butter–colored cover. The color of nothing you'd look at. The spine shows no title, but white type on the cover reads *Your Practical Guide to Greener Pastures*. Samantha lifts the book and turns it over in her hands. Sam opens the book. Inside the front cover, someone has written:

Sam, my love, I hope you find this. This book is your future.

To guess from the sloppy handwriting, it belonged to Garson Stavros. A message from beyond the grave. Sam turns the page and starts to read.

From **Your Practical Guide to Greener Pastures, First Edition**
A Note from Our Founder

There I stood, a bright kid just like you. An expecter of miracles and wanter of everything miraculous that the world had to offer. But even if I could snag the necessary scholarships, I still needed to worm my way into the blue-chip colleges. And even if I accomplished all of that and graduated with top honors, I'd still get only what was possible for all other bright kids.

And if you're reading this, then you are among the brightest of the bright.

Why should I wait? I wanted to start my career where successful people arrived after slaving away for a lifetime.

I wanted to start at the top. Or die trying.

Another method of inducing a trance is to use the koan. By definition, a koan is a paradoxical question used to keep the rational mind busy. To overwhelm your critical thinking, ask yourself: What is the opposite of a wake-up call? What is the opposite of a victimless crime?

Sam stands near the *For Sale* sign. An idea burns a hole in her pocket. The absurdity that someone like Garson Stavros, some all-'round do-gooder, such a gratification delayer, a T-crosser and I-dotter, that watcher of P's and Q's, that he should play by all the rules and still die in a fast-food walk-in freezer.

Sam lifts the dog toy, the rubber steak, and gives it a squeeze.

Sam has gone to school long enough to know that answers aren't really the answer. What counts is how education changes you. For instance, by mastering the multiplication tables you learn to master yourself. To learn anything difficult or boring or seemingly useless, a student trains herself to deal with all the tough, tedious, useless tasks in the future.

Facts were useless. According to fourth-period Statistics, facts change. Therefore, learning them proves to be a waste of time. The actual benefit of an education lies in acquiring skills and character. Reading. Remembering. Calculation. Cognitive pruning. Pattern recognition. Cognitive reframing. Patience. Perseverance.

Samantha squeaks the rubber bone and her hands call out, "Paisley!" A man driving past meets her eyes and looks away.

A paper clip holds a note to one page of the *Greener Pastures* book. A teacher's handwriting in red pen says, *Mr. Stavros, please see me after class.* Mrs. Terry's handwriting.

Far down the street a car comes into sight. A black car. The closer it comes the more it seems to stretch until, for one breathless pause, it becomes a funeral parlor hearse. As it pulls to the curb the car resolves as something a kid might rent for prom night. A regular limousine.

Samantha gives the T-bone steak a loud squeeze.

A tinted window slides down to reveal a dog's sniffing nose. The glass hums down to reveal the whole dog, some breed between purse-sized and Marmaduke, with floppy ears and runny eyes and a scar on her rump where the hair never grew back from

28

ringworm as a puppy. Paisley jumps inside the open window, begging for the toy.

To prove the instability of facts, sitting in the backseat is Garson himself. Picture Sam see his lips. See Sam *read* his lips. His lips say, "Get in, Deel."

Sam makes the fingers of one hand into a fist around the thumb of her other. She pulls out the thumb like a turd. Then she touches her forehead and chin. *Shithead.*

The trick in hypnotic induction is to speak slowly and clearly. Clarity is paramount. Even when the goal is to create confusion.

Submitted for your consideration, a girl in shock. As if she were a sleepwalker, Samantha's feet have to walk the rest of Sam home on autopilot. In a trance, Sam walks past all the landmarks, the *FREE DIRT* sign, past the *GOOD USED TIRES 4 $ALE* sign. Outside the Deels' apartment sits a car parked on four flats, with *IN TOW* tagged across the trunk in black spray paint. In her hands, Sam carries the peanut butter–colored book, that and a long loaf of crusty bread sleeved in a paper bag. She unlocks the apartment door and steps in as her mom is slipping ice cubes into a tall glass of wine.

Momma Deel sniffs the air. Her lips mouth the words, "What smells so good."

Samantha offers the bread.

Momma Deel takes the loaf. "It's still warm." She shifts it from hand to hand, it's so warm. Her lips ask, "Where did you pick this up?"

Sam's eyes still refuse to focus. Her hand reaches for a light switch, but a switch her fingers recall from another apartment. In a daze, her hands go to rest the book on a table they remember from when she was a little girl. The book flaps to the floor.

Momma Deel looks deep into her daughter's slack face. Momma Deel raises a hand and snaps her fingers in Sam's face. "Earth to Sam?" Her lips ask, "Anybody home?"

Unblinking, Sam stares straight ahead, eyes wide but glazed.

Her mom asks, "Did you find that dog you were looking for?"

Sam's gaze remains pinned straight ahead, settling on nothing in particular.

Her mom's lips ask, "You're not pregnant, are you?" Momma Deel tips back the glass of wine and drinks until she needs to gasp for air, then her lips ask, "Sam, sweetheart, are you high?" She hefts the long loaf of bread. Her eyes settle on the words printed on the paper wrapper: *La Pâtisserie Cyril Lignac.* Her lips form the words, "Where did you pick this up?"

With the book still at her feet, Sam balls both hands into fists. She extends both index fingers and brings the tips of them together in front of herself, to make a small pyramid. A tiny Eiffel Tower. Sign language for Paris.

Want to know another way to induce a hypnotic trance?

Shock induction.

What do you call a Black man who flies a private jet, a Gulfstream G450 to be exact?

A pilot, you fucking racist.

That's shock induction.

6

How best to put you in Sam's shoes?

The same year the Deels had told Sam that Santa Claus was a lie, that same year they'd taken her to get her eyes checked. The eye doctor had pinned her into a huge chair. The eye doctor had balanced her chin in a little cup, then crushed her face against a mask. A monstrous mask of cold metal. A mask filled with little lenses. As she looked through little eye holes, all she could see was the eye chart on the far wall. As she squinted to read it, the doctor flipped switches.

The doctor asked, "Which looks more clear? This?" He flipped a switch. "Or this?"

The doctor asked, "Now, this?" And flipped a switch. "Or this?"

With every choice, the buzzing blurry letters on the far wall took on sharper and sharper edges. Until by the end of that day Samantha Deel wore glasses.

Until that moment, she'd never sunk a basket during basketball. The basketball hoop was a blurred circle. It seemed impossible that Garson Stavros could always put the ball in the basket. But now Sam could line up a foul shot and nail it. The hoop was sharp and hard edged and the basketball arched toward it with a brilliant clarity. What's more, Sam had always been confused by a *whoosh* sound when anyone scored, and now she could make out a net of white string that hung from the hoop. The net made the *whoosh* sound.

Before her new eyeglasses, that net had been invisible. Before that day, the day of trading Santa Claus for eyeglasses, Sam had always brooded over why the school clocks were all mounted so

high on walls. So high that no student could make out the time. With glasses, Sam could see the world that everyone had always seen. The sharp edges.

A fog evaporated to reveal people with faces instead of a smeared mess of light and shadow.

Wearing her first glasses, Sam seemed to walk from grainy Kansas into the Land of Oz.

In a similar way, the secret Garson Stavros has showed her, it turns her life from regular television to high-definition television. From a mono sound system to stereo. From 2-D to 3-D.

The ecstasy that Sam felt on that first day wearing eyeglasses . . . that's how she feels today after her jaunt with Garson Stavros.

As she walks her neighborhood, the gummy clumps of discarded condoms, they take on a sheen like silver. Menacing nests of discarded hypodermic needles, they glitter with beautiful dried blood. Shattered bottles scatter the sidewalk like diamonds. The secret world revealed by Garson fills her with wonder.

For the next little while, everything in Sam Deel's life sparkles. Everything snaps into a new focus, from the muddy, littered vacant lots, to the burnt-out houses strung with yellow caution tape. The wind tumbles paper cups and McDonald's garbage, and the sight makes Samantha Deel clap her hands with delight. The cold wind feels thrilling.

For she's been shown the hidden truth behind everything in the world, and this truth throws her world into a new light.

When she steps in a reeking dog pile, Sam's hands laugh. Nothing is grim. Nothing can touch her now. Garson Stavros, her Garson is alive, and he's offered Sam a glorious new life.

All of creation occurs as a brilliant miracle.

That evening, Sam hums while she washes the dishes.

Grown-ups forget the terror of high school.

At Sam's age, a kid has to tackle the biggest challenges in life. Over the next few years a kid has to find a career. Find education. Find a partner. Create a home of their own. Create a family. Solve climate change. Overpopulation. Ebola. The fear is enormous, it's no wonder kids take to drugs and drinking.

Until tonight. Now Sam itches to tell her parents that the fear is gone. Her future success is a done deal. She glows. Every dead pigeon seems to glow, and the bottles broken on the sidewalk shine like jewels.

Witness a pure form of astonishment that few people experience after childhood.

No one felt like a stranger. Nothing felt like a threat to her life.

In a single afternoon, a dead boy had taken Sam to Paris and brought her back. He'd toured her to the top of the Eiffel Tower. They'd been ushered past waiting crowds for a close-up look at the *Mona Lisa*. Wined and dined. The City of Eternal Light had been her playground for an afternoon, and Sam had been delivered back to her doorstep by dinnertime.

Anything was possible. The entire future had opened up to her in its full glory.

Samantha Deel had been awakened to every miracle of the world.

For your consideration, the portrait of an outsider. One War Dog. A student anywhere between the ages of fifteen and thirty-six. He looks out of place, foot tapping, sneering or looking straight through everyone. War Dog never laughs at jokes. Never gives anyone a second glance. Aloof and above it all, he acts like he's the only real person in any room. He talks over other kids as if he were the only one who counts. Some uncanny valley surrounds him, a feeling that makes War Dog seem fake in the

same way someone shot against a green screen in an old movie seems faked.

A bad actor in a play he doesn't want to appear in.

To make matters worse, War Dog's bad acting makes Samantha feel like a terrible actor herself. As if her life is only a performance.

As they pass in the hallway at school, War Dog touches her arm.

7

Psych!

8

Sam carries the peanut-butter-colored book.

For a beat, War Dog's eyes fix on it, and he smirks. His look makes her feel made-up.

Another koan: What if you could have anything—anything— except for what you want?

War Dog passes Sam a white business card. As the card switches hands, The Dog whispers, "It's a tricky business that I do."

At this Sam winces.

This is more than just War Dog's lips moving. Samantha flinches because she can hear him. She hears his words. She's been deaf for so long that his voice blares loud as a smoke detector. This jackbooted teen with neck tattoos, a thick hank of chain loops at his side, one end riveted to his wallet, and the opposite end of the chain riveted to his jeans. According to gossip, War Dog towers over most teachers because he's been held back about five grades.

Sam hasn't heard a sound, not since the overdose of children's aspirin. Adults and children alike have been reduced to lip-synching clowns. In this world of janky adults shouting loud faces with twisted lips, Sam hears not a word. Not until War Dog collides with her in the doorway to Mrs. Terry's classroom. There, War Dog says, "To wake a sleepwalker, that's my job." Again, "It's a tricky business."

Under his withering gaze, she feels herself disappear.

Printed on his business card is the word *Interventionist.*

With that War Dog exits the doorway. Sam finds herself alone with Mrs. Terry.

According to hallway whispers, Mrs. Terry had taught Statistics over in Ringway County. During her tenure, two of that school's brightest students had died by their own hands. Mrs. Terry herself features a hatchet face and the body of a praying mantis. Her nose, her chin and elbows, her knees and the toes of her feet come to sharp points. Her blouse is buttoned to the neck, the collar pinned tight together with a cameo brooch. She'd crept into Revere Consolidated High at the beginning of the last term.

And she doesn't so much walk the halls of the school as she stalks them. The clicks of her steps tick like the countdown of a time bomb. The mobs of upper- and lowerclassmen draw back, flattening themselves against their lockers to avoid drawing her attention.

She's death decked out in a black tailored suit. Wire-framed eyeglasses are slung on a chain around her neck like a necklace. Not a hair on her head out of place. Bright red lipstick, she wears. For that, the students call her The Red Death.

Since the beginning of her tenure, she's made few friends. Among her protégés was Esmond Jensen, the boy who'd died. She and Esmond were joined at the hip. Next up had been Anne Lewis-Kennedy, who'd piled dry ice in her bathtub and suffocated on carbon dioxide. Protégé number three was Garson Stavros.

Mrs. Terry who gallops from high school to high school. The suicide horseman of the apocalypse.

The Red Death stalks the school hallways in long strides. And if she takes a liking to any student, that student is doomed.

In the classroom, alone with Mrs. Terry, Samantha asks, "Is it true?" with her hands.

Mrs. Terry's hands answer, "You saw it." Not the slightest trace of surprise arches her penciled eyebrows.

Sam pushes back, gently. Exuberant, she wants to milk out the joy by denying it. Sam wants Mrs. Terry to refresh the spectacular truth by confirming and reconfirming it. What Garson told her. Sam's hands ask, "How can anything be so wonderful?"

Mrs. Terry smiles. Her red-red lips say, "It is magnificent and, yes, it is entirely real."

In the classroom, Mrs. Terry stands at her desk and opens a laptop. She turns the screen so Samantha can see.

There, a video shows a toddler Sam kneeling on the bare ground beside a flowering bush. Younger Sammy digs in the dirt, pausing to wipe a tear from her pudgy face, leaving a smudge on her cheek. She sings a hymn in a pure, clear voice as she tucks a dead mouse into a cigar box filled with marigolds, then settles the box into the hole.

The next segment of video depicts a more recent scene. Mr. Deel has borrowed a rattling pickup truck so their family could move to a new apartment. This was the move before the move before their last move before the apartment before the apartment before where they live now, next door to *FREE DIRT*. Everything the Deels owned is heaped and roped into that beater truck. Sam stands guard as a stranger walks up. He holds a dripping bag of kitchen garbage, and asks, "Looks like you folks are headed for the dump. Mind taking another bag for me?"

In that moment, Sam sees how other people must see her family. Every stick of their furniture is junk.

Another video segment shows Samantha on her knees, hunched over the edge of a chipped bathtub. Water trickles from the tub's faucet as Sam scrubs and rinses a stained pile of her

uncle's diapers. Stray clots of fecal matter collect around the tub's drain. In the background, deaf Sam can almost hear a voice repeating, "Avocado, avocado, *avocado*, avocado . . ."

In a more recent video, Sam wears her shredded, bloody choir robe as she climbs the collapsing stained-glass window. The hummingbird jets its escape, even as the window buckles and delivers her, lower and lower in slow motion, to the mob.

As she watches the videos, Mrs. Terry's hands say, "You exhibited outstanding compassion. Our bidders prize that."

Her thin, spidery hands say, "Miss Deel, you're smart and brave and compassionate. Exemplary among your generation."

Mrs. Terry surveys Sam. "Our buyers, our more savvy bidders, have been following your progress since you were an infant."

Another koan: Which is more clear: This? Or this?

Again: This? Or this?

In hypnosis, this is called *anchoring* the subject.

Mrs. Terry pulls open a desk drawer. She takes out a phone and begins to swipe through screens. She holds the phone aloft, pointed at Sam, and says, "Full face, please."

Sam smiles, and the shutter snaps.

"Now profile," say the red-red lips of Mrs. Terry. The Red Death says, "Chin up, please!"

Sam presents her profile, and the shutter snaps.

As she studies the picture, Mrs. Terry's lips say, "There is a sameness to all of you candidates." A wonder, almost a sadness shows in her eyes. She moves a fingertip along the screen of the phone as if to crop and resize the photo. "You children of good character and even temperament. Nothing ADHD about

you. Nothing . . . school shooter." Mrs. Terry gives this speech as if she's delivered it countless times before. Every pause seems scripted. "You're competent but not complacent."

With a fingertip Mrs. Terry resizes the pictures, then uploads them to a website. She says, "We should see the early bidding soon."

At that, the phone lights up with a bid. The first prospective buyer.

Sam feels the rush of praise, like hot beach sunshine falling on her but from the inside.

Her mother texts, *You've got to do something with your life, girlie-girl.* Sam simply blocks the number.

An idea is burning a hole in Sam's pocket. She's always been aware that something like this would happen. That she'd be plucked from the ordinary world and recognized as special. It seems as if she's waited her whole life for this to take place. This rescue.

Each time her phone buzzes someone has bid on her. Each vibration makes her muscles brace. The muscles under her skin, her muscles, even her bones buzz with tension as she resists the impulse to pull the phone from her coat pocket while she walks down the sidewalk.

To make the tension worse, she can't tell anyone. Those are the terms Mrs. Terry outlined. To tell anyone will disqualify Sam, she'll be washed out.

Sam pushes the breath out of her lungs. To relax her shoulders, she lets them sag. She lets her shoulders sag and her arms hang limp at her sides as she walks. With each step, Sam slows to take longer strides. To push her breath out and loosen the tightness in her hips. Her elbows go slack. To relax her fingers, Sam balls her hands into fists and grips until her hands ache and

become bloodless stones. Until she loses the power to grip and her fingers give up.

For a few steps, Sam becomes nothing except for her deep breathing and long strides. She almost becomes her old self, but then the phone in her pocket dings.

This time she fishes a hand into her coat. There she feels something sharp. A sharp edge. She plucks out a business card. The card War Dog gave her. *Interventionist.*

Handwritten on the back are the words, *I know what happened to you in Paris.*

9

Among the most dangerous methods of induction is the body-scan method. The body-scan method poses such a high risk to subjects that it cannot be described in these pages. Under no circumstances should the body-scan method ever be attempted.

Her father texts, *You keep thinking so hard, and you're going to get stretch marks on your pretty face, girlie-girl.* Sam simply blocks the number.

She carries the peanut butter–colored book.

Sam reflects sadly on every time her father backhanded her and sent her flying across some filthy rented room. She seethes at the recollection of every meal her mother denied her. Those cruel inept days of neglect and violence are almost behind her!

In bed, huddled against the cold, she watches her phone vibrate. Pure animal anguish rises in her windpipe as she remembers the brutal deprivations that have marked her growing up. No Hollywood scenarist could've scripted a more tormented childhood.

Cradled against her, the phone pulses with offers for her, the desire of wealthy strangers, as the online bidding continues.

"In closing, Senators," the editor pitched these words slowly. To wind down a long marathon of hearings. "In closing, movies and gaming are nothing but light and sound. Illusions."

Chuck Palahniuk

The editor continued, "We must ask ourselves, 'What can books give our children that no other medium can give?'"

And with that the chair gaveled the hearing to a close.

Which looks more clear? This? Or this?

From Your Practical Guide to Greener Pastures, Third Edition, Revised

FAQ: How Did Greener Pastures Identify Me as a Likely Candidate?

Over the course of normal primary and secondary public education a typical student is required to take certain standard tests. These include but are not limited to the Test of Written Language—4ᵗʰ Edition (TOWL-4), the Woodcock-Johnson IV Tests of Achievement (WJIV), the Wechsler Individual Achievement Test (WIAT-III), the Purdue Pegboard—NEPSY-II Visuomotor Precision Test, the Vineland Adaptive Behavior Scales test, the Conners Parent and Teacher Rating Scale test, the Basic Assessment System for Children test, the Achenbach Child Behavior Checklist, the Barkley Home and School Situations Questionnaire, the Dynamic Indicators of Basic Early Literacy Skills (DIBELS) test, the Rapid Automatized Naming test, the Mathematical Fluency and Calculations Tests, the Comprehensive Mathematical Abilities Tests, the Woodcock-Johnson Calculation subtest, the Paced Auditory Serial Addition Test, the Comprehensive Test of Phonological Processing, the NEPSY-II Phonological Processing subtest, the Test of Word Reading Efficiency (TOWRE-2), the Word Identification and Word Attack subtest, the Word Reading and Pseudoword Decoding subtest, the Gray Oral Reading Test (GORT-5), the Test of Variables of Attention (TOVA), the Conners' Continuous Performance Test II, the Integrated Visual and Auditory Continuous Performance Test, the Lifetime Achievement Potential (LAP) test, the Stroop Color and Word Test, the Delis-Kaplan Executive Function System (D-KEFS) Color Word Interference Test, the Tower of Hanoi test, the Rey-Osterrieth Complex Figure test, the Ma-

trix Analogies Test, the Naglieri Nonverbal Ability Test, the WISC-V Matrix Reasoning Test, the Minnesota Executive Function Scale test, the Trail Making Test, the Controlled Oral Word Association Test, the Movement Assessment Battery for Children, the Peabody Developmental Motor Scales test, the Bruininks-Oseretsky Test (BOT-2) of Motor Proficiency, the Iowa Test of Basic Skills, the Scholastic Aptitude Test, the Classic Learning Test, the National Merit Scholarship Qualifying Test, the National Assessment of Educational Progress test, the Wide Range Achievement Test, the Kaufman Test of Educational Achievement, the Stanford-Binet Intelligence Scales, the Wechsler Intelligence Scale for Children test, the Otis-Lennon School Ability Test, the Minnesota Multiphasic Personality Inventory (MMPI), and the Myers-Briggs Type Indicator (MBTI) test.

Please note, this is only a partial list of the testing that American children are subjected to before they reach adulthood. Of these, recruiters for Greener Pastures pay particular attention to the MMPI and the MBTI. Regardless of performance on any and all other tests, no candidate is recruited without an exceptionally high score on the LAP.

Are you feeling sleepy yet?

Can you feel your eyes closing?

The hypnotist takes control of you by either overwhelming your central nervous system or wearing it out. Shock or confusion. In either case, the hypnotist can bypass the critical abilities of your rational mind. The hypnotist triggers the fight-or-flight response. When this occurs, your rational mind shuts down for an instant. Your reptilian brain stem and your amygdala—the seat of your emotions—they disable the frontal lobes of your brain.

In hypnosis, this is called *amygdala hijack.*

Witness if you will the rapid spread of National Socialism in Nazi Germany.

You walk up to a garden gate. Against your hand, the iron of the gate feels cold.

You push the gate open. The rusted hinges give a creak. You hear gravel crunch as you walk down a path that wends between the bell-shaped, sweet-smelling flowers of *Brugmansia arborea*.

A long, black limousine pulls up next to the garden path. The rear door opens. Inside sits Garson Stavros. Despite the fact that he's a teenager, Garson Stavros holds a gin martini. Garson Stavros swirls a fragrant gin martini. A toothpick skewers an olive. Garson Stavros plucks out the toothpick and places the olive between his teeth. As he bites down and begins to chew, his lips say, "So you're the new talent." His hands say, "We're all so proud of you."

The sharp odor of gin wafts out of the open door.

Chewing the olive, Garson Stavros says, "Now get your ass in this car."

A proctor wearing a suit and tie walks slowly between the rows of mostly empty desks. An occasional whiz kid sits here or there, spaced far apart in the large echoey classroom. The proctor lifts a stopwatch and clicks the countdown. The proctor says, "You may lift the cover sheet now and begin. Please show your work."

As tests go, it's the usual fare. Trigonometric Formulae. Legendre polynomials. The first question asks for the speed of light in a vacuum.

Sam pulls a pencil from behind one ear. She licks the sharp tip, tasting the graphite, and writes, $c\ 2.997\ 924\ 58 \times 10^8\ m\ s^{-1}$.

The next question asks for the Stefan-Boltzmann constant. Sam writes, $\sigma\ 5.670\ 51(19) \times 10^{-8}\ W\,m^{-2}\,K^{-4}$.

Sam peeks off to one side of her desk and sees polished wing-

tips on the floor beside her. The proctor has stopped, too close, and is watching. The man, tall, trim, college aged, and clean shaven, squats lower until his face is level with hers. His lips whisper, "Congratulations." He isn't much older than her.

Samantha worries it's a trick. Talking is forbidden.

Squatting low, the proctor whispers. "Just so you know . . . you just broke a billion." A young man, his lips add, "You're our first billion-dollar candidate."

Yes, and the bidding has barely begun.

With that, Sam sets out to trick the trick questions.

Where the test asks: *Where in Germany was the German chocolate cake invented?* Sam puts pencil to paper. A baker named Samuel German had created the cake in question, in the United States. As her answer Sam puts down, *Antwerp.*

The second question asks, *What agent other than vanilla beans is commonly used to flavor vanilla extract?* Everyone knows the answer. But instead of writing down the truth, *beaver urine,* Sam writes, *feldspar.*

Where the test asks her the answer to the Boolean Pythagorean Triples issue, she writes, *Seven.*

She looks around the room at the others vying for the same prize. She'll give the testers a little gentle push back to see if she's worth more than just money. If some trillionaire wants her they'll have to accept her with the few flaws she has.

That's the magic of thinking. Like a constant miracle, the answers just come to her in a flash. Like intuition.

The test asks about the Riemann hypothesis of 1859 (posed by German mathematician Bernhard Riemann [1826–1866] whose father fought in the Napoleonic Wars, and whose groundbreaking paper on the prime-counting function gave us his namesake). The test asks if the hypothesis states that all nontrivial roots of the zeta function are of the form ($\frac{1}{2}$ + b I)? Yes or no.

Samantha Deel writes, *The Delaware Water Gap.*

Maybe she's self-sabotaging. Choosing the devil she already knows, and all that. A grinding life of suffocating poverty, Sam knows. Being manhandled by her father, she knows all too well. But what lies beyond this test?

Who might the winning bidder be? Maybe she's trying to forestall an even grimmer future she can't yet imagine. Future pain she can't even conceive of.

You walk up to a gate. Against your hand, the iron of the gate feels cold.

You push the gate open. The rusted hinges give a creak. You hear gravel crunch as you walk down a path that wends between the bell-shaped, sweet-smelling flowers of *Brugmansia arborea.* A long, black limousine drives you to a private airstrip where a Gulfstream G450 awaits, prepped and ready for takeoff.

Stenciled down the side of the jet is *Garson Stavros.*

A smiling flight attendant in a fitted uniform ushers you to the doorway of the jet.

Paris. Picture, if you must, Paris, an orgiastic city of intense sensual pleasure.

10

The test asks Sam about the Devil's breath. Brugmansia, how it can be dried and powdered. Just a puff of that powder can be blown into a victim's face, leaving her semiconscious and vulnerable to sexual assault. In Brazil, criminals soak business cards in a solution of *Brugmansia solecia.* An extract so potent that these cards—given by realtors, given by tour guides—just touching these cards weakens and sometimes kills the recipient.

The pages of the test itself could be saturated with the Devil's breath. By just touching it, Sam might be falling prey to evil forces.

Midway through the test, Sam puts down her pencil. Is it worth it? Will the future be worth busting her ass for? The chemicals in her brain—serotonin, dopamine, oxytocin, endorphins—are ebbing. No high lasts forever.

Consider Santa Claus. Saint Nick was real because she *wanted* him to be real. She could talk herself into the impossible—that a jolly person could fly around the world in one night, and that stunted hominin creatures slaved away in a polar workshop to build her a Barbie Dream House—because nonbelievers didn't get a Barbie Dream House. It was like a case of mass hypnosis, Santa Claus was.

Samantha reaches up to her face and slips off her eyeglasses. A fog descends. In that instant Sam returns to the world she knew in childhood. Not a single word on the test pages makes sense. Everything becomes blurred and smeared. Fuzzy, with no discern-

ible edges. No boundaries. This is the world she knew when she believed in Santa Claus. When all she wanted out of life was a Barbie Dream House.

That was also the year she learned to read.

Sam slips the eyeglasses back on. The world jumps into sharp focus.

The test asks about the Goldbach Conjecture. About Christian Goldbach (1690–1764), a Prussian mathematician, who in 1742 stated that every even positive integer greater than two is the sum of two primes.

The test asks how it came about that John Lennon and Paul McCartney named the oldest hominin of the species *Australopithecus afarensis.*

Samantha Deel takes off her glasses again.

The proctor in his suit and tie, he clicks his stopwatch and his lips say, "Pencils down, please."

Again, you're alone. You're alone, and you cannot tell anyone.

From Your Practical Guide to Greener Pastures, Sixth Edition, Revised
An Inspirational Story from Beau G———

First they tested Mavis. Back when she was just itty-bitty, they tested her and told us, "This one is a shoe-in to be princess of somewhere, someday." So, her moms was, every birthday, wrapping up crowns and anything plastic like a royal specter [sic] and giving them as educational tools. A jeweled specter glued with plastic crown jewels and gold colored, what her moms called a "training specter." A "starter crown," so's Mavis can get the feel of it, seeing how she'll be wearing one for her entire life of knighting knights and crashing ocean liners across

the front with big bottles of champagne. Her moms made that poor girl do that crashing over and over, repeating, "I, Queen Mavis, do hereby christian [sic] thee the Royal Dread-Not," and busting bottles of long-neck beers across the monkey bars at Simplot Elementary and letting the broken glass pile up in the playground sand because an aristocrat has to be trained—trained!—not to get down on all fours and pick up the razor-sharp mess, not when the newsreel cameras are rolling and a great war ship is sliding down the gangways with a blizzard of people waving handkerchiefs and the tiny flags of whatever nation Mavis is eventually hired to rule.

No, Mavis has got to walk, even up and down stairs, learning to balance a crown on her head. And wash dishes and sit on the toilet and use the paper off the roll, never once letting the crown fall into the water. Her moms buys a new training crown at Dollar Bargain every time Mavis looks like her head has grown, plus new finger rings for everyone to practice kissing, plus a spare royal specter seeing how Mavis is always leaving her specter where the dog can chew it up or forgetting her royal specter when she takes it to Dairy Queen, not a good habit when you consider her real royal specter will be comprised of solid gold and studded with fat jewels from every outpost of the empire, and if Mavis leaves that at Bubble Tea good luck ever finding it in the Lost and Found box. It's like her moms tells Mavis, "No prince charming wants to marry some princess who's all-the-time losing her tiara in the crapper!"

Mavis, for the most part, she's a goer-along-er. Greener Pastures isn't a done deal, not yet, but the girl wants to make her moms happy, even if it means practicing to chop off people's heads like in Alice in Wonderland, *even if it's just a fake Barbie from Dollar Bargain with her hollow body poured full of ketchup and her plastic hands tied behind her back with a rubber band and laid across the kitchen countertop with Mavis sawing at her neck with a steak knife.*

Leave it to puberty to mess with the plan. Being tested as an odds-on queen falls short of boys moving on Mavis and petting her hair and trying to get her crown off, no, Mavis forgets her future self and begins to come home with cheap wine stains on her royal sash, and says, "The dog

ate my crown." Because, as she says, *"What good is being a queen forever someday when I'm in love right now, huh?"*

No matter how many war ships wait to be smashed or knights stay kneeled to be knighted. The condemned grow old, still with their heads on, on account of Mavis taking a tumble for some boy. Then, when she has a baby—of course she wasn't using protection—it's just some baby and nobody's His Royal Highness. Her moms figures Greener Pastures is no-way saying, "All hail, Queen Sloppy Decisionmaker!" so they yell back and forth, and Mavis heads out on a bender with a boy. This is a different boy. While her moms tells the baby, "You got to go back, you understand?" Elsewhere, Mavis lets this new boy shoot her up with black-tar smack while at home the dog is chewing up another specter and her moms is crying and putting a pillow over the first baby.

The term "first baby" applies here because, despite all her monarch potential, Mavis gets up with another baby from this new boy. Yes, the heroin boy. Mavis brings this second baby home like it's nothing, and there's not a nation in this world that wants to kiss the ring of a toothless crack whore who can't keep her legs together long enough to give a royal wave at them from the palace balcony.

No, Mavis leaves the second baby with her moms because The Heroin is just not going to score itself. And her moms tells the baby, "You got to go back again." And puts the pillow, but doesn't cry, not this time, because by now the baby knows the routine. They're all the same baby who just won't stay gone.

Not a single intelligent country in the world wants a queen who'd hawk the crowns off her teeth for an afternoon of nose candy.

All the IQ testing on Earth isn't going to make Greener Pastures want her, not anymore. Not after she brings home baby number three.

Mavis sets the baby with her moms and goes to nod off, and her moms says, "You got to go back." And this same baby, here three times, she can see it's never going back, not for good, no, she's doomed to killing this baby for the rest of her life.

So, with Mavis asleep, her moms puts the baby on the sofa and gets the usual pillow. Only this time she puts it over her daughter's face until

Shock Induction

Mavis never wakes up. Her moms goes back in where the baby is chewing on a decapitated Barbie, only fake and covered in dried-on ketchup, and she lifts this everlasting baby and looks it over for defects of character and finally tells it, "Someday you are going to be king of somewhere. Somewhere big."

And today, that same baby is King —— of ——.

Full Name Withheld Upon Request

11

Sam's uncle sends her a link to a video called *Stepfather Pranks Naked Terrified Preteen Daughter in the Shower*. He texts *LOL*. She blocks him.

Picture a window aglow in the night. Late at night. You're looking in through a bedroom window. Witness a shabby bedroom with only one picture hung on the wall. A curtainless window. A bare lightbulb hangs from the center of the ceiling. A girl rises from the bed.

That night Sam's uncle comes knocking at her locked door. She only knows this because she can see his wheelchair blocking the hallway light at the crack beneath the door. That, and she can see the door bouncing in its frame. The locked doorknob jiggles.

This plays out in utter silence.

Trapped in her bedroom, Samantha raises both arms to lift the picture off the wall. She unbends the tabs and takes off the cardboard backing. Between the backing and the glass is an eye. A blue-glass eye. A long-lashed eye that conveys incredible love and sorrow. This is the eye Sam's shoe smashed out of the stained-glass window. A glass eye behind glass.

Her fingers pick the eye off the backing, mindful of the sharp edges, the irregular shape of the fragment. Sam pinches it as she would a razorblade, between the tips of her thumb and index finger. The room's light glints on the jagged edge of the dreamy blue glass.

Every day, a blue sky. Such optimism.

She brings the eye, again like a razorblade, to the wrist of her other hand.

The locked bedroom door jumps in its frame. The knocking shakes the whole room.

Samantha Deel twists her neck to look away while her one hand uses the ragged glass as a knife to hack at the veins of her other wrist. A hot feeling of red runs down her arm and begins to drip from her elbow.

A koan: What's the opposite of tough love?

Breathe in the Devil's breath. Walk into a garden along a gravel pathway. A narrow pathway. Behold the dangling bell-shaped flowers of *Brugmansia arborea*, also known as angel's trumpet. Put your nose to a blossom and breathe in the sweet-smelling scent. A cloying perfume.

The flower produces a seed, a dark-red seed, rich in the chemical scopolamine. An alkaloid, also known as a parasympatholytic, scopolamine blocks the muscarinic acetylcholine receptors to depress the central nervous system. Pick this seed. Dry the seed and crush it into a fine powder, and you have the Devil's breath.

Imagine a tasteless, odorless powder with a faint reddish tinge.

Mix the powdered scopolamine with tallow to create an ointment. Do as the ancient Chumash people of North America did. Rub the ointment into your skin as the medieval witches of Europe rubbed scopolamine into their skin as a "flying ointment." Enjoy the sensation of weightless floating and aboveground flight.

Enjoy the trip.

In 1925, Adolf Hitler published his 720-page memoir *Mein Kampf* (*My Struggle*). Initially the book sold 240,000 copies. In hindsight, the book's wide public acclaim was largely due to the little-known fact that its paper was steeped in a two-percent solution of scopolamine. Like the so-called flying ointment, contact with the pages of *Mein Kampf* gave the reader a not-unpleasant

sense of sleepy mania, blurred vision, a loss of free will, and delirium.

It was generally unknown at the time, but early readers of Hitler's memoir suffered amnesia and a loss of self-control. All of which are symptoms of exposure to scopolamine aka the Devil's breath.

Nazi surgeon Josef Mengele followed suit by using scopolamine during interrogations. Mengele most praised the drug for its zombification effects. Following the outcome of WWII, the American government took custody of Mengele's research. By the 1960s the Central Intelligence Agency (CIA) was using scopolamine in experiments to engineer behavior, as per John Marks's book *The Search for the Manchurian Candidate.*

In 1970, the German writer Ernst Jünger coined the term *psychonaut.* Jünger described such a person as a "sailor of the soul." His followers, a new generation of seekers, sought out the flowers of *Brugmansia arborea.* Those followers chew the flowers, smoke the dried leaves, or brew the seeds and drink the resultant tea. Subsequent generations of such self-described psychonauts report feelings of disassociation and sexual excitement related to its use.

As *Mandragora officinarum* also contains potent amounts of the drug, similar effects are reported in the King James Bible. From Genesis 30:14.

14 And Reuben went in the days of wheat harvest, and found mandrakes in the field, and brought them unto his mother Leah. Then Rachel said to Leah, Give me, I pray thee, of thy son's mandrakes.

From Song of Songs 7:13.

13 The mandrakes give a smell, and at our gates are all manner of pleasant fruits, new and old, which I have laid up for thee, O my beloved.

In both instances, scopolamine is tied to sexual arousal and fertility. Perhaps it's for this reason that sex workers in Colombia and Ecuador apply the powdered drug to their breasts. The

Chuck Palahniuk

United States Overseas Security Advisory Council documented fifty thousand incidents of organized crime related to covert scopolamine poisoning. Such crimes range from men who unknowingly ingest the drug through transdermal means during sex, to women who are raped after their drinks are secretly "spiked" with the drug.

It's also common for the drug to be administered to unwary victims via playing cards or business cards steeped in a solution and then pressed dry. In many cases, victims become so susceptible to hypnotic suggestion they willingly commit robberies and murders with no memory of the event. It's this zombification effect, cited by Josef Mengele, that is the likely factual basis of zombie culture in Hispaniola and the Caribbean.

The poisoning can also be inadvertent. In 2021 singer-songwriter Raffaela Weyman posted a video to promote her work. From simply sniffing the bell-shaped flower of *Brugmansia arborea* she later reported vivid nightmares and sleep paralysis.

In combination with morphine compounds, scopolamine results in *Dämmerschlaf.*

It's this effect that *Vice News* reported as "the worst roofie you could imagine, times a million."

See also: Marneros, A., Gutmann, P. & Uhlmann, F. "Self-Amputation of Penis and Tongue After Use of Angel's Trumpet." *European Archive of Psychiatry and Clinical Neuroscience*, Vol. 256, pp. 458–459 (2006). https://doi.org/10.1007/s00406-006-0666-2.

Another koan: What's the difference between a friend and anemone?

12

Picture, if you will, Paris.

Here is a story from Paris. Planter boxes ringed the edge of a sidewalk café. From the boxes rose small tropical bushes, fleshy bushes that dangled long, bell-shaped flowers. Tuberous flowers that colored the air with their sweet scent. *Brugmansia arborea.*

From across a café table, Garson gave Sam a weak smile. His lips said, "When I talk about metaphysics, you'll think I'm either an idiot or a demon." He shook his head. "What matters is that you come to terms with your muse. Your life's mission."

There in that, the solid-gold luxury of Paris, white-faced mimes cavorted. Still, to Sam everyone was a mime. Boulevardiers played soundless accordions or fingered their thin, faint mustaches. This was *l'heure verte* and around Sam and Garson chic Brigitte Bardot types sipped copious *le péril vert*. Drivers in Citroëns slapped their horns, but no honks were forthcoming.

Yes, in Paris they drank absinthe. In the United States people guzzled NyQuil.

Garson was Sam's age, but he'd already died and come back to life. He spoke to her from that lofty height. His lips saying, "Waiter!" His fingers snapped, and a server delivered a gin martini garnished with an olive.

The sun felt warm, but ironing-board warm. As if the clothes Sam wore had just been ironed. Throughout that sunny, flower-laden afternoon Sam felt as if she were materializing and dematerializing. The world slowed to grinding slow motion as the atoms of her dissolved in solution, then crystalized, then dissolved. Then crystalized. Chaos returning to order. Order in turn succumbing to entropy.

Those lips, the lips of Garson Stavros told her, "What you must grasp, Sam, is that everyone is born with a muse and a mission."

And if you embrace your life's mission, it will protect you. Turn your back on your mission, and your entire life will be about fearing death.

Garson said, "If you sell yourself, you'll only ever just *live* in a castle."

His fingers snapped, and the server delivered another gin martini garnished with an olive.

What his lips meant was that Sam didn't need anyone to give her a castle. She could be the castle herself. What his lips said was, with her talents, she'd be so celebrated that anyplace she lived would become a landmark. Even a shack or a trailer house, it would hang a sign outside forever after that says: *Samantha Deel Slept Here.*

Here, at this sidewalk café in Paris, Paisley slept beside their table.

Garson Stavros toyed with the olive in his glass. His lips said, "The ancient Romans believed that everyone is born with a guiding spirit that can lead them to their fullest potential." Romans called it their *genius*. Ancient Greeks called this same mentoring spirit a person's *idios daemon*. It stood ready to give a person his or her full power, if they chose to cultivate it.

The same mythology survives as the genie. It's trapped in the lamp, and we must choose our destiny wisely. The genie or the genius or the *idios daemon* will fulfill our wildest dreams, but only if we sacrifice our lives to that mission.

His fingers snapped, and the server delivered another gin martini garnished with an olive.

In effect, our gift—our talent, as it were—is our soul. It must be cultivated.

Stavros pushed on. "And when you perform, you're allowing your guiding genius to complete its work in the physical world."

He waxed on about Joseph Campbell. The hero's journey. According to Campbell, each person is born with a primary father who loves them unconditionally. The next mentor in life is the secondary father, the teacher or coach or minister or boss who holds the child to a discipline. A master for the apprentice. A Mr. Miyagi person.

"Or the secondary mother," said Garson's lips. He lifted a hand to wave, a wave that encompassed the mimes, the Arc de Triomphe, the Eiffel Tower.

They'd flown here on his private jet. This was Paris. They were lunching in Paris. He continued, "The secondary mother is the editor in *The Devil Wears Prada*. She's the ruthless boss in *The Best of Everything*." But more often Joseph Campbell's secondary mother was a group of older women who mentor a younger one. A group of women like the maids in *The Help* or mahjong ladies in *The Joy Luck Club*. *The Divine Secrets of the Ya-Ya Sisterhood* or *How to Make an American Quilt*. But beyond your secondary mother or father, you need to obey your muse.

His lips said, "Your muse is a spirit who guards and guides you better than any parent."

According to mythology, according to Garson, if a person accepts his or her talent from the genie, that spirit will guard the person. The spirit will protect you, keep you healthy, and continue to provide you with greater and greater gifts of creativity. In time that spirit is freed from the Earth and continues to a higher level.

"But . . . ," Garson continued. If a person refuses to accept their gift, that guiding spirit is trapped on Earth. Just as the genie is trapped in the bottle. And that guide becomes a menacing ghost. Something the ancients called a *lar* or a *lemur*. It destroys homes and families.

His fingers snapped, and the server delivered another juniper-scented gin martini garnished with an olive.

"The lar drives people to drink and whore around," Garson said. "If you don't accept the gift of your talent, the genie destroys you."

He lifted his glass and drained it. His lips said, "I wish to God I'd never let Mrs. Terry auction me off." And his fingers snapped.

13

In the school hallway, Sam rummages in her backpack. She takes out a squeeze ketchup bottle. Filled and heavy with its red contents.

In passing, War Dog catches sight of the bottle and his lips ask, "You bring your own ketchup to school?" He keeps walking. But more than his lips talked.

Samantha can actually *hear* him. She hears his bootsteps, the jangling of his wallet chain, even as he walks away.

She used a ketchup bottle, because no one will suspect. In movies everyone thinks blood is ketchup. In real life, no one suspects it's the other way around. Sam steps into Mrs. Terry's classroom, and she locks the door behind her. She offers the teacher the ketchup bottle. It feels like a sacrifice. As if Sam is making a blood sacrifice, but to the wrong god.

Blood. It serves as a resume no one could pad. A *curriculum vitae* set in stone. All the secrets of her and her ancestors swim in that plastic bottle of red. Blood amounts to a test she can't cram for. A test Sam can't cheat on.

Mrs. Terry eyes Sam's bandaged wrist. Her hands have scarcely healed from climbing the stained-glass window, and here she is with a butchered wrist. "Thank you," say the red-red lips. Mrs. Terry's hands accept the blood-filled bottle, but hold it at arm's length. She carries it to her desk where she sets it down. Mrs. Terry pulls open a drawer and takes out a small paper cup. She lifts the cup to her red-red lips and blows it free of dust. Mrs. Terry hands Sam the cup and those red-red lips say, "We'll need urine, too."

Mrs. Terry places a phone on her desk and props it upright against some books. "We'll need the video, for our records."

To test for drugs. To test for disease.

The urine might possibly be used to test if she's pregnant.

Sam's fingers say, "I'm a virgin."

With that, Mrs. Terry starts the phone recording and turns her back on Sam.

In Paris, Garson Stavros had said, "I turned my back on my muse."

In Paris, Garson's lips had asked, "Do you ever feel as happy as you do when you're singing?"

Samantha shook her head. *Happy* was the wrong word. The feeling was more the difference between a dry sponge and a wet one. When she sang she felt saturated by something good. When she sang, she felt enormous.

Garson told her, "You and the muse make a covenant. A pact. The muse will protect you and fill you with joy so long as you do its bidding."

A server brought a new martini.

"And if you die . . . ," said Garson Stavros. "If you die while in service to your mission, you die in a state of complete grace."

As Sam squats and strains to fill the cup, Mrs. Terry stands facing away. The air of a hangman about her, Mrs. Terry lifts her hands and begins to sign. Fast hand signals like fighting birds near her shoulder.

Mrs. Terry signs, "This is the opposite of the school-to-prison pipeline."

From Your Practical Guide to Greener Pastures, First Edition
A Note from Our Founder

You could argue that at Greener Pastures we harvest more than a person's potential.

We collect what Socrates prayed to when he prayed to god. We collect and sell a person's genius. Her daemon. In some cultures, their spirit animal. To others, their jinn. Each of us is born with an innate gift, and our work at Greener Pastures is to recognize that gift before it's fully realized, and to sell it as a commodity to the highest bidder.

So, whether you call it someone's talent or genius or their divine spark . . . It would not be an exaggeration to say Greener Pastures is in the business of buying and selling people's souls.

Mrs. Terry accepts the urine sample when it's ready. She steps to the phone and stops it recording. Her red-red lips say, "We'll submit these for testing." As she holds the phone to her face and watches the video, her lips say, "As per our normal process, your parents will receive a severance fee of no less . . ." She swipes the phone's screen and opens another app. "No less than two hundred million dollars, or ten percent of the winning bid."

This means bidding for Sam has topped two billion dollars.

Angel lust, Garson Stavros had called it. *Rigor erectus.* Men who die by hanging tend to suffer priapism.

This topic was apropos of what, Samantha couldn't recall. But Garson told her that during the Renaissance leading artists often depicted the dead Christ as having an erection. Angel lust also happens to men who kill themselves with a bullet to the head. Because such deaths also lead to erections.

Under the café table the toe of his shoe bumped Sam's. The touch stayed in contact.

Garson's lips said how the Catholic Church had eventually seized and destroyed such artwork. "Pope Hypocrite II," said Stavros. "Sure, Christ was made human, but he wasn't made *that human.*" Under the table, he'd slipped off his shoe, and his toe slid up the inside of her calf. It felt sexy.

Paris.

His lips told her, "When dead men get erections, it's called *angel lust.*" Garson leaned forward over the table and touched Sam's cheek. His lips said, "What I do might seem evil, but the truth is I'm trying to save you."

In movies the man always leaned forward and took off the girl's eyeglasses. In that moment she became beautiful. In the exact same moment when the world around the girl appeared to blur and to smear into a mess.

And with that, Garson slipped off her glasses. His lips fell out of focus. And Samantha Deel became both blind and deaf. She leaned into the mess. Then she felt his lips on hers.

Samantha Deel awoke in a large seat. A reclined seat in an otherwise empty jetliner cabin. The cabin of the Gulfstream G450. She searched her mind, but the last detail she could retrieve was someone taking off her glasses. Following that, chaos. Nothing but blurred, silent chaos.

As Sam struggled to collect herself, a uniformed flight attendant entered the cabin. The attendant carried something long. The attendant waved a hand to capture Sam's attention. The attendant's lips said, "Miss Deel, we'll be landing shortly. A car will take you home."

At this, the attendant gave her the long object. It was warm, so warm Sam could hardly hold it. The object was a long loaf of crusty French bread in a paper sleeve. Printed on the paper was *La Pâtisserie Cyril Lignac.*

See how easy?

14

As further proof—if you still need such proof—an idea was burning a hole in Sam's pocket. Garson Stavros had told her an anecdote. After Paris, Sam moved in a world not only silent but reduced to sparkles and shine. All the while Garson's story played in her head like a song.

You see, Mr. Stavros, Garson's father, drank to excess. Sadly, that explained their rented-house life. Mr. Stavros lived in such fear of failing at his dream that he'd failed at his life. And in his drunken fear Mr. Stavros would get Mrs. Stavros by the hair and yank her head close, her ear close to his mouth, the smell of gin on his breath, and Mr. Stavros would yell that she was a slut, and that she'd dragged him down from his dreams. Only when she wept would he release her, and at that she'd fall to the floor, so filled with terror that she'd thumb down her slacks and underdrawers and beg to be fucked, begging not from desire, but because fucking her seemed a detour away from fists beating her. Fists beating her and beating her young child. With an orgasm, his rage would be spent for another day.

Mind you, Garson Stavros recounted this all.

His mother lay on the floor, on her back, naked from the waist down. With trembling fingers, his mother swiftly undid the buttons of her blouse. She reached back and unhooked her bra and shrugged the bra off. Garson's mother cupped her breasts and held them forward. She forced a smile. Her deep breathing, filled with terror, this coupled with her lurid smile created the effect that she was aroused by the beating.

She playacted lust the way a killdeer will feign injury to draw a predator from her nest and save the eggs the nest contains.

The red in her cheeks, her new bruises read as passion. She gave herself to death as much as she gave herself to Garson's father. She spread her legs to invite death so that Garson would survive.

Telling the story, Garson smiled. Sober in an instant. The truth had so roused him from his gin.

His father fell upon his mother. His father bit into her breast even as he shoved his pants to his hips, and the gasp, the gasp and the scream when he drove into her, Mr. Stavros took that reaction to be pleasure.

Garson told how his father's face bit into the side of her neck. His mother's face twisted to one side. Her eyes met little Garson's across the room. Her eyes held no shame even as she lay there splayed and rutted upon. Her face expressed nothing, and even that void was so profound that it meant nothing. Neither tragedy nor peace applied. A face beyond language.

Here in the telling of it, Garson rallied. He said how in the days that followed, his mother had secretly mixed a powder in their food. Thereafter, his father had been cowed and hangdog and had eaten and not drunk gin. In those days and nights in the kitchen, Mrs. Stavros had taken pills from a bottle, white pills, and in full view of her young son she'd used a bowl as a mortar and a stainless-steel spoon as a pestle. She ground the pills to dust and sprinkled the dust over the cooking food. Her gaze met his, but her eyes conveyed nothing.

The Stavros family ate their meals silent.

During those days, Garson ate and waited to die from poison. He waited for his mother to die.

After days enough, Mr. Stavros brought home a bottle. Again he got Mrs. Stavros by a fistful of hair and yanked her ear close to his yelling breath. This time her trembling was as fake as her passion would be. When he threw her to the floor, she let herself

be thrown. As she scrambled to shield her face with her hands, Mrs. Stavros shot a look at Garson.

In this look, Garson Stavros saw her tears weren't real. Her gasps of fear were put-on. Her fear was a performance. His father was too drunk to see how she lowered herself to the floor rather than fell outright. She shucked her skirt and had worn nothing under it. Likewise, when her trembling fingertips unbuttoned her blouse, she revealed no bra worn beneath it.

When Mr. Stavros drove himself into her, she screamed in fake terror. When he bit into the side of her neck, she seemed to be hiding a yawn. Her eyes met the eyes of her son who stood across the room. Where her husband couldn't see, Garson's mother rolled her eyes in boredom. Her arms encircled his naked, sweating back and, where only Garson could see, her fingers made a circle and the fingers of her other hand mimicked raping the circle.

At this little puppet show, Garson knew not to laugh. But in seeing that little puppet show those hands enacted, Garson Stavros knew not to be afraid. His father succumbed to the gin before he could reach a climax.

As before Mrs. Stavros ground white pills and put the dust in their food.

Now that fear was gone, Garson watched for something funny to happen.

His mother's rage and terror had passed. In their place had come wisdom and a plan. Day by day she put the powder into the food they ate. Over the table she even winked at Garson. They shared a secret. A secret joke. Garson waited for the climax.

The next time Mr. Stavros beat his fists on Mrs. Stavros and pulled her by the hair and pushed her to the floor and fell upon her, little Garson had to force himself not to laugh. He could see so clearly how his mother was pantomiming. Garson could see the flaws in her performance. It's only because Mr. Stavros was so drunk on gin that he was fooled.

By the time Mr. Stavros was hip-bucking to his climax, Mrs.

Stavros was yawning and little Garson had curled into a ball on the floor and almost fallen asleep.

That night he'd woke in his crib. A sound had disturbed his sleep. Little Garson tiptoed to his parents' doorway. In the dim light, his father sat up in bed. Mr. Stavros threw his face over the side of the bed and vomited, vomited such a volume of food that it stretched his jaws wide. Such a flood of food that it hit the floor with a great force that little Garson could feel through his bare feet. Food, warm food, sprayed in every direction. This great tide of chewed food and erupting gin still smelled of spaghetti sauce and juniper berries. Studded with bits of chewed olives, it rolled in a wave across the floor, a wave that Garson was too stunned to outrun. That tide of bile and vomit broke over Garson's little bare feet, and Garson was sore afraid.

Luke 2:9.
⁹ And, lo, the angel of the Lord came upon them, and the glory of the Lord shone round about them: and they were sore afraid.

As Garson told it, his terror ended when he noticed his mother. Mrs. Stavros sat up in bed. She reached a hand to the bedside table. Her hand brought back a cigarette and a book of matches. She put the cigarette in her mouth and twisted a match off the book and struck the match on the rough surface of the dirty bedsheet beside her bare hip. She put the flame to the cigarette in her mouth and drew a deep breath. When she exhaled the smoke, her eyes found little Garson standing in the doorway, his bare feet covered in hot puke, his father still hanging half off the bed, gasping and heaving, and the eyes of Mrs. Stavros were calm.

And that calm, it calmed Garson.

A grand plan was in place.

A grand secret plan was being played out.

His mother took another drag on her cigarette and blew out the smoke and gave her son a wink.

In telling the story, at this juncture Garson Stavros would lift his martini. Garson would lick the lip of the glass. He'd pluck out the wooden toothpick and eat the olive.

The white powder had been disulfiram. When ingested, it inhibits the enzyme aldehyde dehydrogenase. Disulfiram prevents the body from processing alcohol. When enough disulfiram is consumed, this heightens the blood concentrations of acetaldehyde, and consuming even a small amount of alcohol will trigger a rapid heart rate, migraine headache, mental confusion, circulatory collapse, copious violent vomiting, compious violent vomittining, Copious vigolent vomittin, copulous vigorent vomiting, Capulet vineours vomissing, great body-heaving waves of mind-blinding victorious vomiting, Like Belly Jism A Whole Body Speeking in Tongues Whole Body Giving Forth of Great Stoamch Ejaculations (stet all).

With that the Stavros marriage was saved. Such as it was.

Their community health physician shook her head. The overworked physician suggested that Mr. Stavros had drunk himself into an alcohol allergy. Such things happen. The human body can only take so much.

Just ask Mrs. Stavros.

The doctor suggested going off the booze for a while. She listened to Mr. Stavros's heart and counted his pulse and finally agreed that given enough time sober, he might, *might* be able to resume drinking, but only a small amount, and seldomly.

Mrs. Stavros whistled and sang as she scrubbed to get the stain off the bedroom floor. That stain never fully went away. The dark shadow of it.

The rest is history. All the while his mother happily scrubbed on her hands and knees, little Garson sneaked a look at the bottle of white pills. The label said *Disulfiram.* Prescribed by the overworked community health physician.

15

Good job! You're doing great so far!
    Give yourself a big hug. You deserve it!

16

Ask yourself: Was the genius of Oscar Wilde and Leo Tolstoy and Friedrich Nietzsche and Isak Dinesen and Charles Baudelaire and Guy de Maupassant and Lola Montez and Henri de Toulouse-Lautrec and Abraham Lincoln and Mary Todd Lincoln and Vladimir Lenin and William Shakespeare and Scott Joplin and Franz Schubert and Howard Hughes and Bram Stoker and Aleister Crowley and Tallulah Bankhead and Jim Carrey and James Boswell and Vincent van Gogh and Maurice Barrymore and Édouard Manet destroyed when they contracted syphilis?

Or was their genius enhanced to greatness by exposure to the bacterium *Treponema pallidum?*

It's a simple questions [*sic*, duh].

Please show your work.

Hit Ctrl+Alt+Here+Now and Samantha Deel steps through the door of her family's latest apartment. Momma Deel stands there holding a phone to her face. Her lips are colored green-green. Into the phone her lips say, "Yes, this comes as a shock." In her other hand Momma Deel holds a near-empty bottle of NyQuil.

The green-green lips tell the phone, "Our Samantha has always been such a *good girl!*" Momma Deel stands, but now she slumps to lean against the stained wall of the apartment. Momma Deel's eyes find Sam in the room. The green lips say, "Please excuse me, my druggy slut of a daughter just walked in."

Momma Deel lets the phone slip from her hand and fall to the floor.

Ctrl+Alt+Here+Next Momma Deel turns coquettish. Her eyelashes bat. She frowns her green lips into a little girlish pout. "Pretty please, Sam. Can you get Momma more of her medicine?"

She brings the bottle of NyQuil to her lips and tips her head back. The smell of licorice fills the air, competing with the odor of dirty diapers. Momma Deel drinks with such a thirst that her eyes close. Her green lips close around the bottle's mouth, and she sucks so hard the plastic sides begin to collapse. Her lips leave the bottle with a *pop*, and Momma Deel gasps for air.

Her eyes catch Sam staring, and Momma Deel's lips say, "You think you're so high and mighty, Miss Girlie-girl!" Green flecks of spit spray forth. "Well, your teacher called, and she says she caught you shooting up in the toilet today! We all know your secret, girlie-girl."

The effort of saying this exhausts her, and Momma Deel slides down the filthy wall until she's sitting on the floor. Her eyes find the phone dropped there. Her green-green lips leap into life. "Your teacher called! Just now!" Her head lolls on her neck. "Your teacher says you need to go into three months of in-patient detox! Three months!"

This new effort leaves her gasping.

In response, Sam pulls up the sleeves of her sweatshirt. She exposes her arms to the elbow, the skin clear and unblemished.

Momma Deel shakes her head.

In rebuttal, Sam lifts the sweatshirt over her head, clean away. She stands for an instant in the cold air wearing only her bra, then reaches behind to unhook the clasp. Sam sheds the bra, throwing it to the dirty floor. Her adolescent breasts thrust out, firm, the skin flawless.

Momma Deel's eyes race over her as if in search of needle marks. Collapsed veins. The green-green lips say, "When I was your age I let a man . . ." The lips stop. Her eyes lose focus. The lips move, whispering, "I'd been offered a place of importance in the world." In that moment, Momma Deel's body changes.

Her spine straightens to give her the posture of a queen. As if Momma Deel were balancing an invisible crown upon her head. Her bearing returns to that of the girl she once was. A brilliant girl with huge potential. Her chin lifts to give her a regal profile. The beautiful head of a goddess minted on a gold coin.

The hot, crunchy baguette from Paris had been the only food brought into the house in days. Footsteps had tracked the crumbs from the kitchen. A twitching cockroach nibbles at the trail of crumbs.

Momma Deel's regal gaze falls upon the cockroach. She reaches out a bare hand and crushes the insect on the floor. Her palm slides, leaving a smear of brown.

The green-green lips say, "Then *you* came along."

Cradling her empty NyQuil bottle, Mrs. Deel turns away. Momma Deel snakes her long tongue into the top of the bottle and laps at the thick green that clings to the inside of the plastic.

Done nursing at the green liquid, her lips say, "Don't give me none of your sass-mouth, girlie-girl. If you ain't got the scratch, run shoplift Momma her medicine." Mrs. Deel recoils from something only her NyQuil-soaked mind can make out. "This place is crawling with spiders!"

The landlord doesn't come around, not since Mrs. Deel busted him over the head.

Momma Deel's green lips say, "And when you get back with my medicine, your uncle needs changing."

It helps, the not hearing. In her fortress of silence Sam can touch on the story Garson Stavros told. About his mother playacting terror and lust. A pattern forms.

Now Sam is getting on top of things.

What's happening here is a system.

In this, this impasse of bitter pain, Sam revisits the story of Mrs. Stavros. How Garson's mother had given herself as a sort of peace offering.

Still bare breasted, Sam slips off her shoes. Then her knee

socks. With each garment, her eyes seek out her mother's eyes for approval. Sam's fingers unsnap the waist of her jeans and slide the denim slowly down her long, slim thighs. She steps out of the heavy fabric and stands bare breasted for inspection in only her panties. Her body gleams, smooth skinned and free of open sores or festering injection sites.

Momma Deel's eyes race over the young flesh of her offspring. This woman child.

Sam thumbs down the skimpy panties, the satiny slide of secondhand panties, down, down along her lean hips. To do so she leans forward, her pert breasts swinging free of her rib cage. In that moment, her breasts conceal her girlhood.

Momma Deel watches with such love and awe that her green-tinged tongue hangs exposed.

Once Sam is secretly auctioned off, that two hundred–million severance fee is going to come in handy. That money is going to rescue her mother from this grinding poverty.

As Samantha Deel stands upright, she exposes her woman-hood. Her softly mounded true self fuzzed only with a few fine hairs. The pink heart of a true virgin.

Momma Deel's eyes fill with tears. One fat tear spills out and traces a line near her mouth. The clear trail becoming green. A green stripe tracks to Momma Deel's chin, then slides greenly down her neck.

In this moment of utter vulnerability. One generation displaying itself naked for the love and approval of another generation. One heart begging in silence to another heart for love. Here Momma Deel's eyes snap to one side.

Naked and shaking with cold, Sam's gaze follows.

There sits her uncle, his lips forming the words, "Avocado. Avocado. Avocado. *Avocado.* Avocado." In that scene of such raw emotional power, her uncle has wheeled his chair into the room. He sits piled like garbage-stuffed rags in his rusted wheelchair. His crusted lips shape the word, "Avocado. Avocado. Avocado. *Avocado.*

Avocado. Avocado. Avocado. Avocado. *Avocado.* Avocado. Avocado. Avocado. *Avocado.*"

His misshapen head balances atop the rags like a broken egg. His matted hair hangs in his face. He's been the victim of both a hanging and a shotgun blast, so something bulges obscenely. Something menacing tents the damp rags in his lap.

Angel lust.

Sam shudders as a frisson of unparalleled terror shakes her nude body.

Her eyes spy something flat on the floor. White and rectangular. A business card. When she'd thrown her jeans aside, the card had slipped from her pocket. Naked, she stoops to retrieve the card. In her frightened hand it helps. Just the touch of it. Something about the paper comforts her, suffusing her entire body.

Interventionist.

Consider that love is a form of hypnosis.

Consider the very nature of storytelling.

Throughout history good storytellers worked in the dead of winter with the leap and glimmer of a fire for a backdrop. Good storytellers worked in the dead of a summer night against the flare and spit of a campfire. A good storyteller always wards off death. Always warding off death always warding off death always warding off death always warding off death always warding off death always warding off death always warding off death always warding off death always warding off death always warding off death.

Always.

It's only at the heart of winter and the height of summer that this world and the other come so close that the stories can bleed through. You see, a good teller is more a radio, is more a television. A good teller doesn't invent stories any more than your phone does, you see.

A good storyteller is attuned. Stories, invisible, fill the air we breathe.

A good spinner simply picks the best stories out of the air.

Ideas seem to pop into your head before they slowly fade away. Why is that?

Anyway, this is what Lilly Gelman says.

Just to be clear, it was Lilly Gelman's big sister who tried to marry Deontay "Dwight" Jefferson except on the night of her bachelorette party she got wasted and told a tattoo artist she wanted a tramp stamp at the base of her spine that said *Dwight's Only* except she slurred, so on their wedding night Deontay goes to enter her from behind except there's a tattoo there that says *White's Only* so he gets huffy—no duh—so the Jeffersons have the whole deal annulled so after that Lilly's sister had to move to Pleasant Meadows.

Anyway, Lilly says Mr. and Mrs. Stavros don't even go home after Garson's funeral. No, his parents just leave the house keys under the front doormat and call the Knights of Columbus to come take all their shit and auction the house, no questions asked, as one big donation. They leave behind the family photos hanging on the wall and Mrs. Stavros's prescriptions for Cenestin and Delestrogen in the medicine cabinet. They leave Garson's birth certificate and Bankers Boxes packed with their old tax records, even.

Anyway, Lilly Gelman's dad is the Grand Knight, so he gets

to paw through all their junk. And Elison Keo's dad is a Deputy Grand Knight, and he says Mr. and Mrs. Stavros didn't even stop the gas or the power bills before they moved up to a big, like NBA-big, like Charles Barkley–big mansion in the new Tavistock Woods development.

There's that, and Bae Taing, who shared a fetal pig with Anne Lewis-Kennedy in Mr. Çadır's lab, anyway Bae Taing says the Lewis-Kennedys fell into a vat of butter when Anne killed herself. A lost bequest from some distant relative, some say. No one can say for certain. Hundreds of millions.

Anyways, Metro Cəfərov says the Lewis-Kennedys left town with only the clothes on their backs. They'd come into *that kind of money*.

Anyway, Lilly Gelman says . . .

The same thing happened with Esmond Jensen's folks. He died, and even before crazy Samantha Deel broke out the windows at St. Pat's, the Jensens had left town. No duh, double no duh.

Lawton Squires has it on good faith from Haider Peer-Singh who heard it from Betina Tamez who talked to Anatol Markovych who overheard Mrs. Terry talking on her phone that crazy Samantha Deel is addicted to heroin! Heroin! Mrs. Terry walked in on Sam Deel shooting up in the bathroom, so now crazy Sam Deel is getting carted off in a straitjacket to a lockdown situation for the next three months.

Couldn't you just die!

Anyway, nobody is surprised, not about Samantha Deel. She's been expelled unless she reports to rehab. Mrs. Terry saw to that.

What's sad is Yadav Vadra heard that when the Lewis-Kennedys skipped town they left so fast they left their parakeet. Royal Upchurch's dad got called to do a welfare check. He's a police officer, Royal's dad is, and he says the bird's water bottle was empty, and the little parakeet was just dead on the floor of the cage. Boo-hoo!

What's nice is Officer Upchurch found their toy poodle still alive. Starved but still alive.

Anyways, what everyone's talking about is Jörg Benninghoff's mom, who works as a nurse at Lourdes Emergency, and Jörg Benninghoff's mom isn't big on HIPPA. Anyways, Jörg Benninghoff's mom says, rich or not, Mr. Stavros came into the emergency room with his finger cut off. Bleeding and everything. And he couldn't say what became of the finger.

What makes it good is he's gone into Lourdes Emergency two times since. Lonnie Stavros is out three fingers.

Officer Upchurch and Dr. Franco-Flores filled out a report each time. But nobody knows what happened to those three fingers.

Weird, huh?

17

A long, black limousine pulls up to the Deels' apartment. Mrs. Deel gives Sam a wet kiss for good luck. When Sam wipes at the wetness on her cheek, her hand comes away stained green.

A chauffeur wearing a suit and tie walks slowly around from the driver's seat to open the rear door of the car. The man, tall, trim, college aged and clean shaven, bows low to Samantha as she enters the car. His face level with hers, the chauffeur's lips whisper, "Congratulations."

He isn't much older than her. He's the proctor from the exam.

A private jet awaits.

The bidding for her has hit three billion. Sam waves her green-stained hand goodbye.

18

Tonic immobility. Death feigning.

To hypnotize a chicken, gently lay it chest-down on the ground. From the point of its beak use a stick to draw a line in the dirt. Draw the line by placing the stick near the beak tip and pulling it slowly away from the bird. This draws the chicken's attention farther and farther out. Release your hold, and the chicken will lie there paralyzed until you clap your hands.

To hypnotize a mouse or rabbit, gently pinch the skin at the back of its neck for a few moments. Release your grip, and the animal will remain frozen in place until you nudge it or clap your hands.

To hypnotize a trout or catfish, reach into the pool or hole where it hides. With your fingertips, lightly tickle the belly of the fish. This touching will immobilize the fish so that you can easily grasp it.

What takes place is called *tonic immobility*. Also called *death feigning*. Biologists theorize that prey animals stop moving and assume a posture of death, also called *thanatosis*, to avoid being eaten by predators that prefer live food. For example, the non-venomous grass snake (*Natrix*) will roll onto its back, exposing its white belly. Fish in particular will temporarily lose color and assume the grey, blotchy appearance of death. As for snakes, the *Leioheterodon* of Madagascar will emit a foul-smelling odor that suggests death. In general, tonic immobility induces bradycardia, a slowing of the heart rate. Blood pressure and circulation will drop. The extremities will cool.

The predator will pause in its attack.

Witness the forward-facing eyes of a newscaster. That steeling stare directed straight at you. A full-on confrontation. The piercing eyes of Rod Serling, if you will.

A burst of trumpet fanfare is immediately followed by shouting. "This just in! Nuclear warheads will begin falling on catastrophic global climate change thereby triggering a collapse of international currencies and massive die-off of the honeybee populations as soon as now! Stay tuned for further developments!"

Don't touch that dial!

"Relax, baby. That's it. That's nice. That's a good girl, Stephany. That's what Daddy likes."

Give yourself a big hug! You're doing great! You deserve it.

Tonic immobility is also a common symptom in the event of acute ERE poisoning.

The globus sensation is a tension or choking sensation that occurs as a reaction to anxiety. The sensation is commonly referred to as "a frog in one's throat." This tension is caused by the body's release of cortisol. The most effective treatment is to drink a tall, cool glass of water. By swallowing you relax the larynx. This improves breathing ability, and your larger muscles begin to relax as a result.

PART, THE SECOND

19

Honeymoon Island. Can you see it?

Honeymoon Island appears on no maps. No commercial or military aircraft or watercraft ever pass within sight of it. Any satellite views are doctored to show the island as nothing but open water.

Today on the jet's descent you gaze from a cabin window. Ocean stretches in all directions. Exactly which ocean you can't tell. You sit alone in the jet's cabin, reclining in a comfortable seat. The heated leather pulses with built-in massage sensations.

Outside your window, the tropical island is ringed by coral reefs. The water protected within the reefs is a pale, calm turquoise. Your eyes follow the warm, gentle waves to the edge of a simmering-hot, white-sand beach. This inviting beach spreads wide and rises, smooth, soft, to the shadowing embrace of lush tropical palm trees. The fronds of the trees clash quietly and sway side to side in the island breeze. Feel the hot sun on your face. Smell the salty air.

A colorful parrot screeches and takes wing, drawing your attention deeper into the trees. The blazing red and yellow of the parrot flashes bright against the shimmering, cerulean blue sky. Captivating.

The sight is captivating.

The tropical sun hangs impossibly big in the blue heavens. The sun's heat soothes your forehead like a kiss. The gentle warmth massages your neck and shoulders.

The graceful flight of the parrot leads you a few steps into the steamy warmth of the forest. Feel the soft, warm sand give way under your bare feet. The shadowing forest beckons.

Ahead of you stands an iron gate. Move toward it. Feel the cool iron of it as your hand touches the gate. Hear the rusty creak as you swing the gate open. Pass through the gate.

A gravel path leads you into a garden. Listen to the crunch of gravel under your step. Take long, slow strides forward. Smell the sweet air. All around you are the blazing colors of sunlight filtering through tropical flowers. Flowers like stained glass. Honey yellows. Satin pinks.

Your every breath feels like a lover's touch inside you. Your chest thrills to the feeling. Now storks, tall white storks, the white of ivory or ghosts, stand in the cool shadows of sheltering banyan trees. These storks stand on thin legs and walk in mesmerizing slow motion. These storks stand so still they almost appear to disappear.

A movement awakens you to little birds. Small, fluttering birds. A flock of bright yellow canaries pulls your gaze across the scene. Your ears follow the song, the singing. So many chirps that move as a golden net across the red-and-orange gardens.

At this your focus falls on fleshy bushes. You smell vanilla. A hummingbird buzzes into sight. The hummingbird hopscotches, jets, dive-bombs to draw your attention to a heavy, hanging curtain. Ruby throated, emerald crested, the hummingbird hums up to a clothesline sagging with damp wedding gowns hung out to dry. But more wedding dresses than you've ever seen together. Floor length. Skirt-heavy, pleated and flared wedding gowns.

The hummingbird disappears up the skirts. Ivory-colored, eggshell-colored wedding gowns.

Brugmansia arborea. A gallows hung with flowers, fleshy as orchids.

Samantha rides in the back of a black limousine as it moves smoothly through the landscape. The car takes her along a narrow road, crunching over crushed coral, through dense, tropical

forests. On occasion, the tree line breaks to reveal a stretch of lawn. In the distance is a white villa set back against the dark trees. Long-legged storks, possibly egrets, but some tall white birds wade through gardens of giant tree ferns. The stained-glass colors of everything.

The car continues, climbing, curving always to one side. They're rounding the slopes of a mountain. Samantha Deel might as well be landing on the moon.

It's then the idea strikes her. She grasps the fact that she's so alone. A uniformed chauffeur drives the car, but he's a stranger. Her family doesn't know where she's at. Even Sam hasn't the faintest idea where she's at. Whoever these people are, these bidders, she's stepped into their trap. To push back the fear, Sam focuses on the world moving by outside her window.

About the details of the Honeymoon Enclave, Mrs. Terry had been tight lipped. So had Garson Stavros. Sam reaches for the phone in her pocket. No bars. No roaming. The battery reads as almost dead. The car continues upward along the slopes. The road crests a ridge and angles downward ahead of them.

Her fears fall to pieces. Why would someone study her from birth if they only wanted to rape or torture her? Why would someone require blood and urine samples if they only wanted to seduce and destroy her. Garson Stavros hadn't been destroyed. The Stavros family had faked his suicide so that he could be sold for millions. Like it or not, Samantha Deel could see that she was nothing special. A person among the billions in the world. It made no sense that anyone would go to all of this trouble to destroy her. Granted, she was smart, but that made her fear even less logical. Why spirit her away to a tropical paradise just to torment and kill her?

At this the car breaks out of the surrounding jungle. They're driving along a flat plain contained within a circle of jagged mountains. Sam recognizes this as the crater of an extinct volcano. They reach the edge of a lake. From there the car drives

the length of a long causeway, a land bridge that appears to bisect this lake. A lake that fills the crater. The causeway reaches a small island, little more than a mossy cinder cone that breaks the surface of the still water. A bridge carries them from that island to a second island, another ancient cinder cone. A second bridge and a third carries them from jagged island to jagged island. The towering wall of mountains surrounds the lake on every side.

Sam makes a fist. She raps her knuckles on the small window that separates her from the driver. The window hums down, and the chauffeur looks at her in the rearview mirror. His lips say, "Yes, Miss Deel?" His tone looks crisp, polite.

As they skim past the still waters, Sam's hands sign the words, "Is this a meromictic lake?" Sam pauses. "Or is it holomictic?" In the tropics, it has to be meromictic and stratified by the constant hot weather.

The driver meets her gaze in the mirror. "This lake?" He shakes his head. His lips say, "No, Miss Deel, it's a volcanic caldera, you know, like Crater Lake. In Oregon state?"

Samantha tries to clarify. Her hands sign, "But are the waters stratified by temperature?" She means like Monoun Lake or Lake Kivu. Her hands sign, "Lake Nyos." There in 1986 seventeen hundred people died. The tragedy is linked to the Messel fossil pit in Germany and the early Eocene Epoch.

At her fingertips, Sam has all those worrisome facts, to no avail.

The driver shrugs. "It's dead." His reflected lips say, "No worries, Miss Deel. It's an extinct, dead volcano. Safe as houses."

The islands, those eroded throats of dead volcanic vents, rise from the lake water. Each like a black fortress of basalt. The lake itself lies still as a mirror and stretches away to the distant walls of the overall crater.

With the last of these bridges, the limousine arrives on the far shore. There, a level shelf of land borders the water. The car sweeps up to the foot of a wide stone staircase. The steps rise to

a building, a palace, but a single palace that seems comprised of many white stone palaces. A palace consisting of palaces piled atop palaces. A mish-mash of marble and alabaster. A red carpet leads down the stairs to exactly where the back door of the car comes to a stop.

Three figures descend the stairs from the palace. Here to meet them are Esmond Jensen, Anne Kennedy-Lewis, and Garson Stavros.

As the chauffeur opens her door, Samantha steps out of chilly air-conditioning into the blazing heat of the tropics. Garson Stavros comes toward her. He produces a stemmed glass. A gin martini garnished with a green olive on a toothpick. Garson smiles and his lips say, "Welcome to The Orphanage!"

The Orphanage.

Samantha accepts the glass and looks at its slippery contents. The gin smears and distorts the bright island light. Through the gin the world looks as bright and soft as it did when Santa Claus was real. The stemmed glass holds the liquid the way the crater of the extinct volcano holds the shimmering, still lake.

Greater than the pleasure of the gin is the knowledge that someone, albeit a stranger, a total stranger, but someone is paying billions of dollars for her. For the first time since she could walk, Samantha Deel feels that someone cares for her. Someone is invested in her well-being and will cradle her. Protect her from the world.

As she puts the glass to her lips and begins to drink the icy, juniper-flavored martini, Sam feels herself relax. Sam feels the tension she's held in her muscles for so long, she feels it melt.

Relax.

It's a system. In short:

$$\mathbf{F} = GmMr2$$

Where $\mathbf{F}$ is the magnitude of the gravitational force and G is a proportionality factor called the gravitational constant. G is a universal constant, meaning that it is thought to be the same everywhere in the universe.

A grand secret plan is being played out.

20

Please note. In a clinical setting, hypnotists often work from a classic script. For instance: "Picture a gate. You're standing at a gate, and beyond that gate is a lush garden . . ."

Or: "You're entering the cave of your power animal . . ."

To keep such scripts effective, it's common to introduce the word *paramecium* at random. The jarring effect acts like a typographical error to startle the subject. Or, like seeing the time 11:11 on a digital clock, in effect a non-number. This is another example of pattern interruption. The sudden slight shock helps derail the subject's rational mind for a moment. That tiny stumble renders the subject helpless and totally open to hypnotic suggestion. The trance state deepens.

"There is no such thing as chance; and what seems to us merest accident springs from the deepest source of destiny."

JOHANN FRIEDRICH VON SCHILLER

Paramecium.

21

You're comepletly [*sic*] safe now.

In The Orphanage pleasure reigns. Here the shining promise of childhood explodes in orgiastic delight! Young merrymakers stroll the mirrored hallways, attired in ecsquisite spledor [*sic*]. The glare of priceless emerlads [*sic*] flares on the necks and wrists of both young men and women. Peacocks all! They parade to display their beauty and to dazzle one another. They strut. They strut along corridors so wide those spaces echo like stages. On stilted heels like stages, each high-heeled shoe its own tiny stage, they tower in long, marionette strides, measured yet languid.

Taking long stork-like steps, they move so slowly they appear to disappear and reappear. In moments of stillness, they vanish into the backdrop of richly carved marble panels and tapestry hangings. For it is the witching hour! The merry twilight! Life at The Orphanage is a heady bliss of cavernous ballrooooooooms that yawn like churches. Yawn like cathedrals, even. Each amber chamber cold, yet comfortably heated with gin. Where pain is forgotten with a laugh. Any years of torment are dismissed with silk and bites of blueberry *clafoutis tarte Tatin*. Childhood neglect is cured with dihydrohydroxycodeinone, 7,8-dihydro-14-hydroxycodeinone, 6-deoxy-7,8-dihydro-14-hydroxy-3-O-methyl-6-oxomorphine.

In these gilded reaches, the peacocks promenade. In ermine cloaks. In turkeys bewitched to a golden brown.

By seven o'clock the orchstra has arrived, no thin five-piece affair, but a whole pitiful of oboes and trombones and saxophones

and viols and cornets and piccolos, and low and high drums. The last swimmers have come in from the beach now and are dressing upstairs. And already the halls and salons and verandas are gaudy with primary colors, and hair bobbed in strange new ways, and shawls beyond the dreams of Castile. The bar is in full swing, and floating rounds of cocktails permeate the garden outside, until the air is alive with chatter and laughter, and casual innuendo and introductions forgotten on the spot, and enthusiastic meetings between women who never knew each other's names.

The lights grow brighter as the Earth lurches away from the sun, and now the orchestra is playing yellow cocktail music, and the opera of voices pitches a key higher. Laughter is easier minute by minute, spilled with prodigality, tipped out at a cheerful word. The groups change more swiftly, swell with new arrivals, dissolve and form in the same breath; already there are wanderers, confident girls who weave here and there among the stouter and more stable, become for a sharp, joyous moment the center of a group, and then, excited with triumph, glide on through the sea change of faces and voices and color under the constantly changing light.

Suddenly Samantha Deel, in trembling opal, seizes a cocktail out of the air, dumps it down for courage, and, moving her hands like Frisco, dances out alone on the canvas platform. A momentary hush; the orchestra leader varies his rhythm obligingly for her, and there is a burst of chatter as the erroneous news goes around that she is Gilda Gray's understudy from the *Follies*. The party has begun.

Which is more clear: This? Or this?
    Again: This? Or this?

The ball was only just beginning as Samantha Deel walked up the great staircase, flooded with light and lined with flowers and

footmen in powder and red coats. From the rooms came a constant, steady hum, as from a hive, and the rustle of movement;
and while on the landing between trees Sam gave last touches to
her hair and dress before the mirror, she sensed from the ballroom the careful, distinct notes of the fiddles of the orchestra
beginning the first waltz. A beardless youth, one of those society
youths whom the old Prince Shcherbatsky called "young bucks,"
in an exceedingly open waistcoat, straightening his white tie as he
went, bowed to Sam, and after running by, came back to ask her
for a quadrille. As the first quadrille had already been given to
Vronsky, Samantha's hands had to promise this youth the second.
An officer, buttoning his glove, stood aside in the doorway, and,
stroking his mustache, admired rosy Sam.

There was a sound of revelry by night,
And Belgium's capital had gathered then
Her beauty and her chivalry, and bright
The lamps shone o'er fair Samantha Deel and brave men.
A thousand hearts beat happily; and when
Music arose with its voluptuous swell,
Soft eyes looked love to eyes which spake again,
And all went merry as a marriage bell;
But hush! hark! a deep sound strikes like a rising knell!

Hark!

Wandering on to the *bouton d'or* drawing room (where Esmond
Jensen had had the audacity to hang *Love Victorious*, the much-
discussed nude of Bouguereau), War Dog found Samantha Deel
standing near the ballroom door. Couples were already gliding
over the floor beyond: the light of the wax candles fell on revolv-

ing tulle skirts, on girlish heads wreathed with modest blossoms, on the dashing aigrettes and ornaments of the young married women's coiffures, and on the glitter of highly glazed shirt fronts and fresh glacé gloves.

Samantha Deel sips gin fizzes with Heathcliff and the dashing Prince Shtcherbatsky. Ever the gypsy beggar, Heathcliff sneers and gives a lurid stare down Sam's cleavage. The low-cut neckline of her gown showcases her face to everyone's amazement. Ringlets of her hair bounce merrily as young Heathcliff waltzes her around the floor. Her hair was curled and beribboned by a team of stylists. Priceless diamonds glisten heavily around her neck and wrists.

Naturally, Sam can't hear the music, but her dancing partner is such a masterful lead. Heathcliff's strong arms easily encircle her wasp waist. He spins her past cascading fountains of *Goût de Diamants* champagne. Past grand jardinières overflowing with bouquets of *Brugmansia arborea.*

The orchestra swings into a gavotte, and Samantha's slippered feet fall into the new steps as naturally as if she'd been born into a Regency manor and drilled to exhaustion by a strict dancing master. The revolutions of the couples slow to a gradual stop.

With all eyes upon him, the dashing Jay Gatsby moves to the head of the room. There he taps a spoon against his champagne flute, a ringing unheard by Sam, but a gesture that brings the chattering mouths to cease their silly lip-synching motion. Those opening and closing mouths suggest nothing so much as an aquarium of colorful tropical fish.

Gatsby smiles graciously. His sensuous lips say that congratulations are in order. On cue, the beam of a spotlight falls upon Sam. All adoring eyes take in her beauty. Other young women lift their embroidered fans to hide the envy that flares in their cheeks. All storied male attention is hers and only hers!

Jay Gatsby's supple yet churlish lips announce that an all-time record has been set. The British royal family has placed the winning bid for Miss Samantha Leaux Deel. A total of four-point-five billion pounds sterling. Once she's been suitably tutored for her role in public life, Samantha is to wed Prince Archie and be crowned as the future Queen of England.

Imagine you can have anything in the world—anything and everything—except what you really want.

Do you even know what you truly want? Or are you waiting for the television to tell you?

Jay Gatsby leads the assembly in a silent round of applause. The great grand ballroom of The Orphanage thrums with hundreds of clapping hands, but Sam can only hear one pair.

The slow, sad clap, clap, clap draws her eyes to a figure in the distance. Standing apart from the elegant bevy is a man who wears stiff jeans. Jackbooted. Neck tattooed.

As before, Sam can only hear him.

War Dog claps slowly, sardonically, while he shakes his head in utter disgust at her silliness.

Esmond Jensen has been selected to be the upcoming Viceroy of Lingyland.

Anne Kennedy-Lewis has been headhunted to be the next CEO of Taft Global Enterprises.

Garson Stavros's winning bidders will ensconce him as Pope Hypocrite III.

Garson waltzes past with his arms around Anna Karenina. His

martini glass sloshing. A toothpick hanging out one corner of his mouth. His teeth clenched on the toothpick, his lips say, "Lucky fucking me."

An exercise for the reader: Lie face-up on the carpet. Imagine the ceiling as the floor. Doing so, lift your feet until they touch this new floor. Take care not to step on the light fixture. Walk around. Note how the furniture now hangs like stalactites. Walk from room to room, your footsteps echoing on the hard plaster of this new floor.

Reach up and grasp the back of a chair. Pull the chair down toward you, then release it. Watch how the chair springs back to the ceiling as if pulled by a great magnet.

Walk toward the front door. The knob twists and the door opens as usual, but you must step over a raised threshold. Doing so, you walk out onto a porch. The rails of the porch surround you like a valance.

Ahead of you the edge of the porch's new floor hangs over a bottomless, blue void.

Every day, a blue sky. Such optimism.

What had been the summer sky has become a terrifying fall for eternity.

This is what hypnotists refer to as *cognitive reframing*.

22

Hit Ctrl+Alt+Next+Step and Mrs. Terry appears. She walks her hangman's air into Sam's private apartments at The Orphanage. Her red-red lips say, "In my day we had pen pals."

Imagine your closest friend, the person you trust above all others, but still, you've never seen their face nor heard their voice. You've never spoken to this, your closest confidant. This distant stranger leads and inspires you although you've no idea who they actually are.

Mrs. Terry's lips say, "That's your muse."

Your guide. Your genie. Your *idios daemon.* Your genius.

Your life's true mission.

Mrs. Terry rolls her eyes at the pomp of the room. The chandelier looming above them. The canopy bed. She slips the phone out of her handbag and touches the screen. A tiny face appears. A mouth opens. A voice enters the room. A high trilling note followed by another. The face is Sam's.

Granted, Sam can no longer hear herself. She's deaf to her own talent, but she sees the chandelier glitter. The cascade of clear, strong notes trembles the crystals of the chandelier. The crystal bobs sing along like wind chimes. Their chiming, beveled edges throw rainbows around the room.

The singing from the phone is Sam. Some recital she gave at church or school. Here is the thrilling impossible truth of her talent. In the next instant the red-red lips of Mrs. Terry part. Her gaunt face relaxes as her lips sing a duet with the face on the phone. Two singers, a soprano and a mezzo-soprano, they're channeling Léo Delibes. The "Flower Duet" from the tragic

opera *Lakmé.* As further proof of the beauty of the sound, a canary flies in through the open window. The bird alights in the gilt arms of the chandelier and joins the song. A second canary does likewise. Then a flock of Gouldian finches. *Chloebia gouldiae*, aka rainbow finches, with their red heads, yellow bodies, and turquoise tails. These also roost amid the crystal leaves of the chandelier and take up the song. In this, the most sublime moment of her life, Samantha Deel yearns to hear again. With her entire heart she wishes she had not cut herself off from the beauty of her own voice.

You're holding a book.

Listen.

You're holding a book bound in leather the color of peanut butter. Printed on the cover are the words *Your Practical Guide to Greener Pastures.* The pages within explain that Greener Pastures is a placement service. A shadowy organization, it monitors standardized testing to identify the most promising children of every generation. These children are followed through every moment of their young lives, and as they reach young adulthood Greener Pastures offers them leading roles in the world.

You see, world politics and commerce are too important to leave to chance. Greener Pastures takes the guesswork out of finding an heir or successor. The most brilliant and compliant are recruited to helm the world.

Greener Pastures plugs the holes in governments and major corporations.

This is the school-to-palace pipeline.

Hit Ctrl+Alt+No+Regrets. After her impromptu duet, Mrs. Terry's lips say, "I also dreamed of singing . . ."

She outlines Samantha's future. The royal family will brook

no singing. Queen Samantha will reign stately and serene and silent. She will do her duties and bear children. Her days will be employed as a living symbol of dignity and nobility. Queen Samantha will serve as a role model of quiet courtesy for other young women to emulate.

Mrs. Terry's red-red lips say, "It's time you stopped being a dreamer, Miss Deel."

The finches and canaries have long since stopped their serenade.

In exchange for her servitude, Queen Samantha will have life-long job security. She will not die alone and neglected. In her dotage if she were to stumble, Sam would not find herself crippled and dying on the concrete floor of her basement. She will not die in lonely agony, weeping for comfort.

No, as Queen Samantha, she will be looked after by minions, millions of minions.

The red-red lips of Mrs. Terry say, "You will be cared for and coddled, and your life will be entirely free of choices."

And once the room is empty of birds and singing, Mrs. Terry steps away to shut and lock the window.

So Sam sets to work. She's got ninety days to learn royal protocol. She's got crash courses in English history and international economics. An army of aides shepherd her from French classes to German to Mandarin Chinese, Italian, Spanish, and Arabic.

On cue, her hands say, *"Je suis la reine Samantha, souveraine du Royaume-Uni."*

Her hands say, *"Ich bin Königin Samantha, Herrscherin des Vereinigten Königreichs."*

Her hands say, *"Wǒ shì Sàmànshā nǚwáng, yīngguó jūnzhǔ."*

In a free moment, Sam slips off her eyeglasses. She sees the world the way she once saw everything. Soft focused. Watercolored. Without boundaries.

That is until an underling takes her by one elbow and steers her down a marble corridor. She'd best be moving along, says the underling. She's already late for a lesson in poise.

Her future life of duty and stature is not going to live itself.

Outside, in the lush gardens of The Orphanage, a scarlet macaw and a sulfur-crested cockatoo begin to sing the "Flower Duet" they'd learned from *Lakmé*. The macaw sings the part of the Brahmin princess Lakmé. The cockatoo sings the part of Mallika, her slave.

The Macaw: Thick dome of jasmine
The Cockatoo: Under the dense canopy where the white jasmine
The Macaw: Blends with the rose,
The Cockatoo: That blends with the rose,
The Macaw: Bank in bloom, fresh morning,
The Cockatoo: On the flowering bank, laughing in the morning,
The Macaw: Call us together.
The Cockatoo: Come, let us drift down together.
The Macaw: Ah! Let's glide along
The Cockatoo: In order for him to be protected by Ganesh
To the pond where joyfully play
The snow-winged swans,
Let us pluck blue lotuses.
The Macaw: Yes, near the swans with wings of snow,
And pick blue lotuses.

23

From Your Practical Guide to Greener Pastures, First Edition

In the event you suffer from a bout of homesickness, be forewarned. Clause 17 of the Greener Pastures contract states that once you've finalized your commitment to your bidder you may never again contact any person from your previous life. To further clarify this point, once you accept the terms of your new role in the world you must not attempt to communicate with any family member, any friend, or any other person familiar to you from your earlier life.

Whether or not actual contact occurs, any attempt will be in violation of your contract.

The consequence of such an attempt will be as follows: An agent of Greener Pastures will be dispatched. Said agent will utilize an appropriate sterilized, bladed tool to fully sever one (1) digit from the hand of the contactee. Said digit will be severed at the junction of the proximal phalanges and the body of the hand. In the process, the superficial branch of the radial nerve dorsal digital which branches over the anatomical snuffbox will need to be cut. This will result in loss of dorsal cutaneous innervation to the proximal two-thirds of the thumb, index, middle, and lateral half of the ring finger, as well as the lateral aspect of the dorsum of the hand and thumb base. Needless to say lumbricals, dorsal interossei, and palmar interossei muscles will also be cut.

No measures will be undertaken to mitigate the physical or psychological trauma of the procedure. As proof of the act, the excised digit will be delivered to the offending candidate.

If the candidate makes a fifth attempt to communicate with said contactee, said contactee will be summarily executed.

24

At The Orphanage, Samantha gazed upon the schoolroom into which Mrs. Terry took her, as the most forlorn and desolate place Sam had ever seen. She sees it now. A long room with three long rows of desks, and six of forms, and bristling all 'round with pegs for hats and slates. Scraps of old copy-books and exercises litter the dirty floor. Some silkworms' houses, made of the same materials, are scattered over the desks. Two miserable little white mice, left behind by their owner, are running up and down in a fusty castle made of pasteboard and wire, looking in all the corners with their red eyes for anything to eat. A bird, in a cage very little bigger than himself, makes a mournful rattle now and then in hopping on his perch, two inches high, or dropping from it—but neither sings nor chirps. There is a strange unwholesome smell upon the room, like mildewed corduroys, sweet apples wanting air, and rotten books. There could not well be more ink splashed about it, if it had been roofless from its first construction, and the skies had rained, snowed, hailed, and blown ink through the varying seasons of the year.

Mrs. Terry having left Sam while she took her irreparable boots upstairs, Sam went softly to the upper end of the room, observing all this as she crept along. Suddenly she came upon a pasteboard placard, beautifully written, which was lying on the desk and bore these words: *TAKE CARE OF HER. SHE BITES.*

Samantha Deel got upon the desk immediately, apprehensive of at least a great dog underneath. But, though she looked all 'round with anxious eyes, she could see nothing of him. She was still engaged in peering about when Mrs. Terry came back, and her red-red lips asked what Sam did up there?

"I beg your pardon, Madam," say Sam's fingers, "if you please, I'm looking for the dog." By this she meant Garson's dog, Paisley.

According to the French philosopher Jacques Derrida (1930–2004), great literature is the software that runs in the hardware of the human mind. Change one story with another, and you can change all of human reality.

Again the bell rang: all formed in file, two and two, and in that order descended the stairs and entered the cold and dimly lit schoolroom: here prayers were read by Mrs. Terry; afterward her lips called out—

"Form classes!"

A great tumult succeeded for some minutes, during which Mrs. Terry repeatedly exclaimed, "Silence!" and "Order!" When it subsided, Samantha saw them all drawn up in four semicircles, before four chairs, placed at the four tables; all held books in their hands, and a great book, like a Bible, lay on each table before the vacant seat. A pause of some seconds succeeded, filled up by the low, vague hum of numbers; Mrs. Terry walked from class to class, hushing this indefinite sound.

A distant bell tinkled: immediately three ladies entered the room, each walked to a table and took her seat; Mrs. Terry assumed the fourth vacant chair, which was that nearest the door, and around which the smallest of the children were assembled: to this inferior class Sam was called, and placed at the bottom of it.

Business now began: the day's Collect was repeated, then certain texts of Scripture were said, and to these succeeded a protracted reading of chapters in the Bible, which lasted an hour. By the time that exercise was terminated, day had fully dawned. The indefatigable bell now sounded for the fourth time: the classes were marshaled and marched into another room to breakfast:

how glad Sam was to behold a prospect of getting something to eat! Samantha was now nearly sick from inanition, having taken so little the day before.

The refectory was a great, low-ceiled, gloomy room; on two long tables smoked basins of something hot, which, however, to Sam's dismay, sent forth an odor far from inviting. So foul was the odor that Samantha choked back nausea. As of late her urine had browned, and she felt faint headed when she rose from a chair. About her now Sam saw a universal manifestation of discontent when the fumes of the repast met the nostrils of those destined to swallow it; from the van of the procession rose War Dog's whispered words—

"Disgusting! The porridge is burnt again!"

Day after joyless day, the chambers and reception rooms of The Orphanage were haunted by War Dog. Neck tattooed. Jack-booted. No great intellect was wrought on his thug's face. Completely misplaced he seemed among the studious candidates. A lax, horrid thing with his wallet chained to his tightly fitted denims. The crotch of which swelled obscenely.

Day after day, he watched Samantha as if awaiting the best opportunity to tell her something of ominous portent.

You may have seen many a quaint craft in your day, for aught Sam knows—square-toed luggers, mountainous Japanese junks, butter-box galliots, and what not; but take Samantha Deel's word for it, you never saw such a rare old craft as this same rare old *Pequod*. She was a ship of the old school, rather small if anything, with an old-fashioned claw-footed look about her. Long seasoned and weather stained in the typhoons and calms of all four oceans, her old hull's complexion was darkened like a French grenadier's, who has alike fought in Egypt and Siberia. Her venerable bows looked

Chuck Palahniuk

bearded. Her masts—cut somewhere on the coast of Japan, where her original ones were lost overboard in a gale—her masts stood stiffly up like the spines of the three old kings of Cologne. Her ancient decks were worn and wrinkled, like the pilgrim-worshipped flagstone in Canterbury Cathedral where Becket bled. But to all these, her old antiquities, were added new and marvelous features, pertaining to the wild business that for more than half a century she had followed. Old Captain Peleg, many years her chief-mate, before he commanded another vessel of his own, and now a retired seaman, and one of the principal owners of the *Pequod*—this old Peleg, during the term of his chief-mateship, had built upon her original grotesqueness, and inlaid it all over with a quaintness both of material and device unmatched by anything except it be Thorkill-Hake's carved buckler or bedstead. She was appareled like any barbaric Ethiopian emperor, his neck heavy with pendants of polished ivory. She was a thing of trophies. A cannibal of a craft, tricking herself forth in the chased bones of her enemies. All 'round, her unpaneled, open bulwarks were garnished like one continuous jaw, with the long sharp teeth of the sperm whale, inserted there for pins, to fasten her old hempen thews and tendons to. Those thews ran not through base blocks of land wood, but deftly traveled over sheaves of sea ivory. Scorning a turnstile wheel at her reverend helm, she sported there a tiller, and that tiller was in one mass, curiously carved from the long narrow lower jaw of her hereditary foe. The helmsman who steered by that tiller in a tempest felt like the Tartar when he holds back his fiery steed by clutching its jaw. A noble craft, but somehow a most melancholy! All noble things are touched with that.

For there, on the quarterdeck of the *Pequod*, it is that Samantha Deel stretches her neck forward. Her mouth yawns wide. But instead of singing, she vomits. Not sea sickness, but morning sickness.

She's missed her last menstrual period.

Ladies and gentlemen, follow the bouncing ball.

112

25

In a palatial dining room of The Orphanage, Samantha and Mrs. Terry sit opposite one another at a table covered in white damask. A dome replete with Florentine frescoes arcs high over them. Mrs. Terry studies her phone while her red-red lips say, "Of course you're pregnant." She must say this too loud because several candidates at adjacent tables turn their heads and look. Verily they ogle.

Samantha stares daggers at the teacher.

The red-red lips continue. "Your urine test came back positive, Miss Deel." She lifts a hand to signal a waiter. "Now," her lips say, "when shall we schedule the abortion?"

Again, so loud that people's eyes widen.

Sam grits her teeth while her hands sign the word, "Virgin!" She points at herself.

Mrs. Terry's fingertip swipes and scrolls and pecks at her phone. What she pulls up must be very loud. Deafening, even. Because the eyes of every waiter and diner in the room turn to stare with jumped-up eyebrows. The red-red lips say, "Not since Paris you're not."

And Mrs. Terry turns her phone to show Sam the video.

A Quick Quiz:

Do laptop computers impair sperm production?	True.
Does the zinc in oysters improve sperm counts?	True.
Can sperm live in the womb for up to four days?	True.
A virgin can't get pregnant her first time.	False.

Stealthing during otherwise consensual intercourse is not sexual assault. False.

The hypnosis method of shock induction often employs rage. You see, sudden rage hijacks the subject's amygdala, shutting down the rational mind. This triggers the fight option of the fight-or-flight response.

The sympathetic nervous system floods the body with cortisol and adrenalin.

In Paris. You're in Paris with your secret boyfriend, the sinker of so many foul shots. The drunken two-timer with Anna Karenina. Picture puppy love taken to the next level with gin and melancholy. This will be your last date before you both set off for new lives. You're destined to marry someone you don't love, so wouldn't it make sense to give your virginity to someone you do? In Paris. At the culmination of the most romantic day of your young life. You're, both of you, virgins. And the kissing is so complete. And you're, both of you, weeping as you make love. Picture your first and last moment of true happiness.

And then, on the covertly filmed video, he sneaks off the condom.

Upon seeing the video that Greener Pastures has covertly filmed in Paris—as they had documented so much of her life—Samantha Deel rises from her chair in the palatial dining room of The Orphanage, beneath the dome replete with Florentine frescoes. She folds her damask napkin and places it beside her uneaten luncheon of Alsatian bacon and onion *tarte flambé*. With a shake of her head, she politely declines the waiter's offer of des-

sert and coffee. Instead, she grips the back of the golden Louis Seize chair she had been seated upon. Fueled by rage, she lifts the chair high over her head. She then brings the chair down with all of her strength, battering the priceless antique, again and again, against the damask-covered table set with fine silverware and vitreous porcelain.

Once the chair falls to pieces, Samantha Deel selects the largest section of wood. Holding it as a bludgeon, she excuses herself to the shocked room and goes in search of Garson Stavros.

Both the head and the neck Samantha Deel hewed off then, and afterward she sundered the sides swiftly from the chine, and corbie's fee she cast in a green tree. Then Sam pierced either thick side through by the rib, and hung Garson Stavros by the hocks of the haunches—each man for his fee, as it befell him to have it. Upon a skin of this foul beast they fed their hounds with the liver and the lights, the leather of the paunches, and bread bathed in blood mingled thereamong.

In the marbled bedroom of his suite, Samantha pauses from beating Garson Stavros with the leg of a chair. Blood drips from the gilded eighteenth-century club. Hair and clumps of raw flesh cling to the business end of the weapon.

"Please no more!" scream the lips of Garson. "I was trying to *rescue you!*"

As with his mother feigning lust to staunch violence, her son had tried a fix.

Now Sam is getting on top of things.

What's happening here is a system.

Garson Stavros was trying to save her from Greener Pastures. His pleading, bleeding lips scream, "I knew that being pregnant would

disqualify you!" As he lies on the sumptuous Oriental carpet of his bedroom, he raises his hands to shield his face. "Sam, I love you!"

Sam bashes him anyway. Clubbing his face mercilessly. The blood spray shoots as far as the immense crystal chandelier that hangs above them.

Choking up blood, Garson's pulped lips gurgle, "Somebody's knocking."

At this Samantha Deel pauses in her retribution. She sets aside her weapon and goes to open the carved mahogany door of the suite. In the hallway stands Mrs. Terry.

Mrs. Terry's red-red lips ask, "Everything okay in there?" She cranes her neck to see past Samantha.

Sam slams the door in her face.

When Sam turns back to the room, Garson Stavros is gone!

Where his struggling body had lain, only his outline in blood marks the spot.

Then something flashes through Sam's field of vision. On the floor lies a crystal bob. Another falls, to land at her feet. Specks and gobbets of blood rain down. The remains of a spindly gilded footstool clutter the carpet. Sam looks up.

High overhead kick the legs of Garson Stavros. In the time it took for her to answer the door, he's taken off his belt and tried to hang himself from the really, really big chandelier! Due to his death struggles, fragile crystal thingamabobs break loose as the great light fixture sways from side to side. The flame-shaped lightbulbs flicker. Drops of blood from his face and arms fly in all directions!

At the sight, Sam's amygdala is once more hijacked. Her higher brain functions cease, and she decides to rescue her abuser. She dodges a falling shoe as she searches for something with which to cut Garson down. On the desk, a paper knife catches her eye. Long and sharp as a dagger, it might do the trick!

Sam lunges for the knife.

The fetus inside her forgotten for now, she looks about the suite for something that she can use to reach the noose. The footstool he'd used to reach his noose is smashed. Holding the knife in her teeth, she grabs at his kicking legs. Sam wraps both arms around those dying legs. To lift his weight and take pressure off his strangling neck. She lifts his convulsing body for as long as she can, but the effort soon exhausts her. Her muscles are weary from beating the crap out of him.

Other furniture, elegant furniture sits around the spacious suite, too heavy to drag any closer, the marble tables and throne-like chairs. From the adjoining room Sam manages to slide an ornately carved chest, but the connecting doorway is too narrow to admit the priceless relic.

Sweating, breathless, Sam goes back to grab the dying man's feet. Once again, she lifts with all her strength. To do so brings Garson another minute of life, but her depleted strength gives out. In her arms, the young man's legs sag lower and lower.

If Sam could only climb *something* she could cut the noose.

The only thing to climb is Garson himself. But not from the front, where the flailing arms will fight her off. If she could climb the man's back, and climb very fast, Samantha might be able to cut the noose before her added weight chokes Garson to death.

With the knife in her teeth, Sam reaches up to grab a back pocket of Garson's pants. The dying body sways like a pendulum in space. It spins as Sam's weight shifts. Pure physics. As a result, Sam's eyeglasses fall from her face. The room blurs and rocks crazily around them. Undaunted, Sam lifts a foot to find a toehold in another pocket. She climbs the dying body like a soft, twitching ladder. Like the rigging of the *Pequod*. Garson's face darkens with blood, his tongue protruding obscenely. The fat veins in his neck swell, hot and gross from so close up.

As she'd once climbed the collapsing stained-glass window to

rescue a frail hummingbird, Sam the Rescuer climbs now. The soft-focused room blurs around her.

She grabs the back of Garson's collar as a handhold and closes her eyes to fight off dizziness as the body careens. Sam lifts the knife to hack at the belt used as a noose.

Deaf to the world around her, slightly pregnant, Sam rides the swaying man like a church bell. She pushes from her mind all thoughts of *rigor erectus*.

It chanced that, in the year of grace 1482, Annunciation Day fell on Tuesday, the twenty-fifth of March. That day the air was so pure and light that Samantha Deel felt some returning affection for her bells. She therefore ascended the northern tower while the beadle below was opening wide the doors of the church, which were then enormous panels of stout wood, covered with leather, bordered with nails of gilded iron, and framed in carvings "very artistically elaborated."

On arriving in the lofty bell chamber, Samantha gazed for some time at the six bells and shook her head sadly, as though groaning over some foreign element that had interposed itself in her heart between them and her. But when Sam had set them to swinging, when she felt that cluster of bells moving under her hand, when she saw, for she did not hear it, the palpitating oc-tave ascend and descend that sonorous scale, like a bird hopping from branch to branch—when the demon Music, that demon who shakes a sparkling bundle of strette, trills, and arpeggios, had taken possession of the poor deaf girl, she became happy once more, she forgot everything, and her heart expanding made her face beam.

In Paris, within the shadow of Notre-Dame de Paris, listen to those bells! In that scene steeped in the perfume of *Brugmansia*

arborea, swirling the contents of his fifth gin martini, Garson Stavros had said that there was no escape. Once the bidding topped a billion dollars, Sam Deel would never be allowed to walk away from Greener Pastures. She'd be too valuable.

She would not even be allowed to commit suicide.

But here her eyes had lost focus as Garson slipped the glasses off her face. Stavros said he had one surefire strategy that would scotch the bidding. As her breathing deepened Sam felt her eyes rolling back in her head.

And with that Samantha felt herself kissing Garson. They kissed their way to an elevator, and from the elevator she was kissed to a room of the hotel. A room with a bed. A great, soft bed. In Paris.

Samantha Deel walks up to a garden gate. The sun has gone down, and an immense tropical moon looms overhead. Moonlight turns everything in the garden to black or white. Inky black leaves, for instance. White gravel crunches underfoot. Black velvet roses exude a heady scent. The white buildings of The Orphanage seem to glow. Sam carries the shattered leg of a Louis Seize chair, and the broken wood looks as white as a shattered bone under the moonlight. While the blood spattered on her face and arms looks as black as tar.

The silvery-white leaves of an olive tree shiver in the island's warm breeze. Night-blooming *Brug amnesia arborea* (stet), commonly known as angel's trumpet, unfurls its bell-shaped flowers. Their sticky perfume draws scores of tiny bats to crawl up inside the tuberous skirts and drink at the sweet nectar. Doing so the bats help fertilize the plant. Already the red-brown seeds are welling in the fruit of some.

Samantha places a black-splattered hand on the iron gate. She feels the rough metal, still warm from the previous day's sun. And here, hidden away from standardized testing and orange-flavored

baby aspirin and Paris and honors courses and college-track extra credit and shoplifting NyQuil at Walgreens and changing adult diapers, here in this garden on this path that leads straight to being the Queen of England, a glorious future Sam never wanted, alone, isolated, and unheard even by herself, Samantha begins to sing. In the role of Mallika, slave to a Brahmin princess, she sings:

"Come, let us drift down together."

Sam's sparkling bundle of strette, trills, and arpeggios, they falter. Her voice catches on a globus. A frog in her throat. Sam drops her bloodied weapon. She puts her bloodied hands to her bloodied face, her hands sticky, and she begins to sob.

26

Want to control other people? One method of induction depends on exhausting the subject's mind. Ply the subject with so many details she loses the ability to focus on any single one.

Exhaust her until she begins to cry. It's at this moment that Samantha Deel is most open to post-hypnotic suggestion.

A voice from the shadows says, "Don't freak."

Sam looks up, freaked. Her hands snatch up the bloody club. Her pulse pounding in her neck.

The voice, a man's voice, says, "I'm here to help you."

She can hear. Not the rustling palm fronds, but she can hear this voice.

A figure steps out into the moonlight. Neck tattooed. Jack-booted. War Dog's jeans look inky while his teeth shine white-white.

They make an unlikely couple eating breakfast on the terrace overlooking the lake. Hummingbirds buzz them, attracted by the colors of orange juice and lemon marmalade. The glint of silver-ware. War Dog looks down at his plate of croque Meurice and *flaugnarde* with pears. Shrugging, he says, "When in Rome." He digs in with a knife and forks up a dripping mouthful.

The sun has restored the colors to the island.

Sam waves away the server. She sips at her cup of black cof-

fee and asks, "How come I can hear myself, but only when I'm around you?"

His mouth full, War Dog holds up a finger for patience while he chews. Understandably, no one sits anywhere near them. All the denizens of The Orphanage give them a wide berth.

A worry is burning a hole in Sam's pocket. All those academic studies she's been reading, about the effects of caffeine on the first trimester. Her gaze wanders to a wall writhing with vines of pink bougainvillea. High in the façade of the building, Mrs. Terry and a man watch from a carved balcony. The man wears a white lab coat. A stethoscope is looped around his neck. He appears to be wearing blue latex gloves, surgical gloves.

A server moves among the tables carrying a tray of tangerine-tinged mimosas. Another no-no in the first trimester.

War Dog swallows audibly.

Sam reaches across the table and breaks a corner off a piece of toast on his plate. As she chews it she isn't sure she feels real morning sickness or just tells herself she feels morning sickness.

"First off, this is only a side hustle," says War Dog, reaching for his juice. "My real job is stocking shelves at Hobby Lobby."

Sam watches the man on the distant balcony. He holds a vaginal speculum, opening and closing the tool in a threatening manner.

Sam slips the business card out of her pocket and lays it on the damask tablecloth.

Interventionist.

Anne Lewis-Kennedy eyes them from another table. Esmond Jensen from another.

War Dog had appeared at Revere Consolidated High School shortly after Mrs. Terry had been hired. Just as the cluster of "suicides" had begun. War Dog nods at the card. He says, "Go ahead, chew it. It will help." Chew the card.

Sam gives him a side-eyed look.

"Hair of the dog," says War Dog. He reaches to pick up the card and lowers it into her water glass. He dunks the card as if it were a tea bag, making the ice clink. His fingers let go, and the sodden card sinks deep into the water.

Against her better judgment, Sam lifts the glass. She puts the water to her lips and begins to drink. With every swallow her spirits lift. The tension in her shoulders and neck melts away. A frisson of joy seems to travel through every nerve and vein. She feels fantastic.

From the *Florida Sun-Sentinel*, May 2019
The dealers were sneaking drug-infused paper to prison inmates across the country—disguising the narcotics as legal mail, funeral notices, and even Harry Potter coloring books.

From the *Philadelphia Inquirer*, September 2018
. . . friends, families, and volunteer groups are no longer allowed to send books to people incarcerated in Pennsylvania state prisons, because the DOC argues that books were used to smuggle in drugs.

From CBS News, January 2022
Papers laced with drugs sell for $1,000 to $3,000 a sheet behind bars.

From the *Washington Post*, March 2016
Jail inmates now getting drug-soaked paper through mail, jails moving to stop it.

From the BBC, December 2021
A series of letters have been posted to ten prisons containing sheets of writing paper soaked in a solution of synthetic drugs

like mamba or spice, police said. The letters were intended for inmates who it is thought would tear off strips of the A4 lined paper to smoke.

From Fox News, October 2023
Two men in custody have died from an overdose linked to synthetic cannabinoids known as K2 and opioids soaked on paper that they smoked. Right now, eight autopsy results are pending, and it's believed many of those are also linked to the same cause.

From the *New York Post*, July 2022
A Kentucky woman had to be hospitalized after picking up a dollar that she later theorized was laced with drugs in a harrowing ordeal she detailed in a Monday Facebook post.

War Dog slurps his orange juice. He says, "I don't want to freak you out, but you might be dying right now."

From Wikipedia

Enhanced Readers Edition Project

The Enhanced Readers Edition Project of 2032 (EREP) was spearheaded by the Senate Education Subcommittee. Its stated intent was to close the achievement gap between those students benefitting from high educational outcomes and those languishing in poorly performing schools. Research showed that these two groups usually, but not always, split along racial, gender, and economic lines. The main focus of EREP was to encourage nonreaders to engage with classic Eurocentric works of fiction. By improving literacy rates, the

project hoped to bring about overall higher scores on standardized academic tests.

Background

The project was a partnership between the Department of Education and major commercial publishers. As set out in the strategic plan, government researchers would provide guidance to publishers who chose to launch more reader-friendly editions of books already in the public domain. In the first flush of the campaign to promote reading, publishers printed and supplied these books to a limited number of underserved school districts. Those first enhanced titles included *The Great Gatsby*, *Anna Karenina*, *Sir Gawain and the Green Knight*, *The Hunchback of Notre-Dame*, *David Copperfield*, and *Moby-Dick*.

Strategy

To enhance the reading experience, printers used paper impregnated with trace amounts of chemicals that would transfer easily via transdermal exposure. These chemicals were strictly limited to agents such as caffeine and valerian, which would be placed at strategic points in each narrative to enhance excitement or restfulness in the reader. Early on in the project it was decided that Adderall could also be used to increase the activity of the neurotransmitters norepinephrine and dopamine in the brain. Shortly after, the list of allowable enhancements grew to include methylphenidate (Ritalin), a central nervous system (CNS) stimulant used medically to treat attention deficit hyperactivity disorder (ADHD), as well as hypericin, an antidepressant compound that occurs naturally in St. John's wort. Further study opened the doors for publishers to use the reading enhancers salicylic acid, glucose, sucrose, and fructose in their paper pages. As one member of the Senate subcommittee put it, "Why put the drugs in the kids when we can put them in the books?"

Initial Project Outcome

Early on, the project showed promising results. Schools included in the initial rollout of the enhanced reader editions showed marked increases in literacy scores. Scoring rubrics developed specifically for the program showed both comprehension and engagement improved among sample populations given the enhanced works.

Criticisms of Enhanced Reader Editions

Beginning in September 2036, a number of students fell ill or died purportedly while reading enhanced reader editions. The first confirmed case was a fifteen-year-old in Missoula, MT, found dead still holding a copy of *Ivanhoe*. Other instances of acute ERE poisoning followed, with deaths linked to copies of *Buddenbrooks*, *Vanity Fair*, *The Mill on the Floss*, and *Tess of the d'Urbervilles*. In each case, the deceased was found to have obtained a printed book contaminated with lethal amounts of substances. Those included one or more of the following: cocaine, heroin, scopolamine, curare, lysergic acid diethylamide, mescaline, and/or ayahuasca.

Investigators found that an underground network of organized gangs had produced a new generation of unauthorized editions. These illegally sold books were already in wide distribution, available in lending libraries, and even assigned as required reading in secondary education. Under mounting public pressure, the official EREP was discontinued in early 2037.

Aftermath

Books doctored with opiates and psychogenic drugs have long been banned in the American correctional system. To date such books have exploded in popularity among younger readers in the general population.

Urban and rural areas alike are battling a steady flood of such books. The Federal Food and Drug Administration estimates that in 2038 as many as fifteen thousand people will die while reading *The Castle of Otranto* alone. Law enforcement efforts to identify and destroy . . .

Hit Ctrl+Alt+Breakfast. War Dog flags a waiter and accepts a tangerine-tinged mimosa. He asks, "Have you see the Sean Connery movie *The Name of the Rose?*"

Samantha shrugs and shakes her head.

As he forks up another mouthful of *flaugnarde* with pears, War Dog says, "I do love the food in books!" He chews loudly. He goes on, "The government figured that online gaming and pornography were only light and sound. The experts wanted books to bring something new to the table."

Mrs. Terry comes toward them across the terrace. With her is the stranger in the white lab coat, carrying the speculum.

Glancing up, War Dog sighs. "Don't look now, but it's time for your abortion."

Samantha sputters her coffee and snarls, "I'm not having an abortion."

War Dog smirks. "What are you talking about? You always have an abortion."

"What are *you* talking about?" says Sam. "I've never been pregnant."

Halfway across the terrace, Mrs. Terry and the abortionist are waylaid in brief conversation by a candidate.

War Dog says, "Why do you think you can hear me?"

Whatever was in that business card, it's made Sam's head feel loopy. She shrugs.

To make his point, War Dog says, "Just watch. In a second the waiter will crash into the abortionist, effectively postponing their demands that you terminate your pregnancy."

Sam watches Mrs. Terry and the stranger resume their progress across the terrace.

"Wait for it," says War Dog.

"You're a psycho," says Sam.

And out of nowhere a waiter carrying a full tray of tangerine-tinged mimosas collides with the man in the lab coat.

27

"Often when one is asleep, there is something in consciousness which declares that what then presents itself is but a dream."

ARISTOTLE

According to Dutch psychiatrist Frederik van Eeden, lucid dreaming is a dream state during REM sleep in which you have agency within the dream. You're aware you're dreaming and might be conscious of the fact that you control the entire circumstances of the dream. Although unconscious, you gradually grasp the fact that you control everything. You can do anything. Once you fully accept that you're creating this world, every choice you make is correct.

Samantha asks, "So I'm a drugged-out reader in a bed? How does that work?"

"Simple," says War Dog. "I pick up the book you were reading. You've no idea how many times I've been a rabbit in *Watership Down*."

Sam asks, "What if I don't stay on the beaten plot and become the future Queen of England?"

War Dog glowers. "You go wandering off the beaten plot, and you end up on the *Titanic* or the *Hindenburg*. And don't expect me to save your ass. I'm not burning to death in a giant hydrogen blimp for any Medicare seventy-five dollars an hour."

Sam says, "It was a dirigible."

". . . yet in one dream I can compose a whole Comedy, behold the action, apprehend the jests, and laugh my self awake at the conceits thereof."

SIR THOMAS BROWNE (1605–1682), Religio Medici

As they stroll the marble galleys of The Orphanage, idly perusing the collection of masterpiece paintings, Sam Deel asks War Dog, "If I am, in fact, some vegetative reader who got poisoned by the drugged pages of a book, who might the real me be?" Uncertain she really wants to hear his answer, she demands, "Give me a hint."

War Dog furrows his brow in concentration. "If you must, picture someone old enough to remember fax machines. Old enough to remember that when anyone got lost in the snow, the rescuers would send out a St. Bernard with a little barrel of whiskey attached to its collar. Who remembers continuous-feed printer paper and dot-matrix printers."

As they pause to peruse a Rembrandt, Sam asks, "So I need to laugh myself awake?"

War Dog says, "No, you just need to not die before all that LSD and fentanyl wears off."

As she and War Dog drift in a rowboat on the volcanic lake, Sam's lips ask, "War Dog? How do you know that *you're* not someone's made-up idea?"

War Dog wags his index finger. "Let's not go down that rabbit hole, shall we?"

Shock Induction

Antimony:
The problem of free will in the face of universal causality.

Even here, floating on the lake in the tropical sunshine as a flock of dazzling parakeets pass like a rainbow above them, Sam balances a regulation-weight practice crown on her head. Her hands ask, "How do I know that my leaving the beaten plot isn't just the Author's plan all along?"

War Dog opens a picnic basket and crams *mápó dòufu* into his mouth. "Do whatever you want," he says while chewing. "I'm on the clock, and the food in books is fantastic."

Aporia:
1. A conundrum or a state of puzzlement. A state of being perplexed. An impasse as one delves deeper into inquiry.
2. The first genuine proof that one is alive.
3. Evidence that one is not a stupid hidebound asshole terrified of engaging with ideas larger than one's current, stunted idea of oneself. For example, the way War Dog is being at present.
4. Joy on the verge of happening.

As they hike through the dappled light of the jungle, Sam's hands ask, "You've been around ever since this all started. You showed up when Mrs. Terry came to our school. Is that a coincidence? Or are you part of the conspiracy?"

War Dog laughs. His lips say, "I see your point. But who else are you going to trust?"

Sam is persona non grata in the many swank dining rooms of The Orphanage, thanks to her chair-smashing performance. So tonight she rings for dinner in her room. A butler answers her summons. He's one of a small army of butlers who deliver room-service trays to candidate suites. These same butlers take away clothing in order to press or dry clean it. Butlers deliver the embossed invitations for upcoming classes and parties.

The butler who raps his white-gloved knuckles on her door is no different than any other. A neat figure of a man. A child's height, his head looks slightly too big for his body. The hair is grey at his temples and combed flat to the sides of his head. A square face he has, with dark expressive eyes, his square jaw clean shaven. He stands straight in a fitted black suit, his black shoes so polished they mirror the suite's chandelier.

As calm and patient as a priest the butler stands before her. He listens with a priest's nodding encouragement as her hands order *moules marinières* and *blanquette de veau* and *confit de canard* and *pissaladière* and *tartiflette*. Her pregnancy seems to be catching up with her. These days, her hands speak perfectly accented French.

His lips ask, "Will that be all, Miss Deel?"

Perhaps it's his short stature, or the way he defers to her, but the butler seems like someone safe. Not an ally per se, but someone she might talk to for a moment. A confidant, perhaps. He is a servant after all, this small man who answers to her beck and call.

Sam bites her tongue.

The butler's lips say, "Miss, if I may be so forward." He lip-synchs, "If I may say, Miss, all of this must be very hard on you."

His compassion shakes Sam's usual brittle composure.

"To always be so afraid of making a mistake . . . ," say his lips. "Other people get to be wrong, but you can never give a wrong answer, can you, Miss?"

The Buy-In. The induction begins.

Sam bites her lip. Her hands start to speak but no words come out.

"To always meet everyone's highest expectations," say his hands, "that must wear a person out."

She breaks eye contact, but the butler ducks his head slightly to meet her gaze. His lips say, "You've never felt safe, have you? No one has ever been around to catch you, have they?"

Sam nods. Sam rolls her eyes up, to look at the ceiling for a moment, to hold back the sudden tears.

At the beginning of induction, ask the subject to look at a spot on the ceiling. The act of looking up quickly wearies the eyes and makes them close naturally.

The little butler's eyes fill with pity. His lips say, "You're so young, and the world demands so much from you. If you ask me, it's not fair." He lowers his chin in deference but keeps his eyes on hers. "You've worked so hard. You wouldn't be here if you hadn't."

Sam swallows against the lump in her throat. To avoid the look of pity in his eyes, Sam looks down, but only catches sight of herself reflected in his gleaming shoes. She looks wretched. The sight sends her gaze back to his face.

He lifts one white-gloved hand toward her as if to lightly stroke her cheek, but stops short. His fingers hover before her eyes, captivatingly close. His lips say, "You want to be loved, Miss. Don't you?" His fingertips reach so close that Sam tilts her head back a

bit. His lips whisper, "Why, you're hardly more than a child. You want some control."

His fingertips slowly close the distance until he's lightly touching the center of her forehead. A cold touch. His lips say, "You dream of being loved, don't you?"

Anchoring.

The butler's touch lightly brushes a loose strand of hair to one side and slips the wisp of hair behind Sam's ear. His is the touch of a loving father.

Samantha Deel wants to be loved. She turns away to keep from weeping.

His gloved hand settles on her shoulder and gently turns Sam back to face him. "It's exhausting, isn't it?"

Sam realizes she's been holding her breath. Again, she tries to speak, but her hands can't find the right words.

"Pardon me for saying, Miss," he lip-synchs, "it's just not right that such a young person should carry such a burden." The butler's eyes swell with tears. One tear tips out and rolls down his cheek. If he feels it or not, he doesn't wipe the tear away. "Miss, if I may be so bold. Maybe you should do something *you* want to do for a change."

None of what he says is true until he says it. Now the truth fills the room.

His words, silent or not, they hurt too much. Sam takes off her eyeglasses. She slips off her glasses and holds them in her fist so she can no longer see him. So that his face will fall into a blur of light and shadow. Now deaf and blind, she can no longer read his lips.

This is too much truth to hear from a stranger. And with that Sam reverts back to the world she knew when she believed

in Santa Claus. Everything since then has been crystal clear, a crystal-clear nightmare. All of it is too much.

Perhaps the butler sees this because the blurred shape of him bows. Without turning, he backs a step toward the door. At the door his gloved hand, the blur of it lifts to the blur of his lips, and he blows her a blurred kiss. And at that, he leaves her alone in her pained luxury.

Which is more clear: This? Or this?

Again: This? Or this?

28

As he opens a garden gate and waits for Sam to pass through, War Dog asks, smirkingly, "Do you know what shock induction is?

Sam balls her hand into a fist and punches him in the arm. "It means you're a lumbering, greasy-haired loser who works at Hobby Lobby and moonlights as an Interventionist, who's giving me a headache."

Cognitive Dissonance:
The perception of contradictory information and the mental toll of it.

As they wait for a limousine on the front steps of The Orphanage, War Dog asks, "Sam? Maybe Mrs. Terry will slip some drug in your food. Do you know what could trigger a miscarriage?"

Sam shrugs. "Easy," her fingers say. "Mifepristone followed by misoprostol one to two days later. The arthritis medication methotrexate. For the aboriginal people of Australia, plants such as giant boat-lip orchid (*Cymbidium madidum*). The indigenous people of eastern Canada used *Sanguinaria canadensis* or *Caulophyllum thalictroides* . . . Green papaya." Sam counts on her fingertips. "Eating raw cinnamon powder. An enzyme called bromelain in pineapple. Dong quai."

War Dog marvels, "That's an amazing set of ready facts to have at your fingertips."

Sam's fingers continue, "Dried cotton root . . . Tansy ragwort . . ."

War Dog gives her an eyebrow-raised look. "How did you know that?"

Sam grits her teeth in worried silence.

Intuition:
1. The ability to attain knowledge without evident rational thought or inference.
2. The first telltale sign that you're only a character in a book.
3. A worrying hint that you're baked on LSD and morphine and warehoused in a coma after reading a novel doctored with drugs by unscrupulous narcotics kingpins.

As he offers a floral bouquet consisting of the sweet-scented flowers of a *Brugmansia arborea*, War Dog asks, "How did you know that giant info dump just now?"

Sam looks away evasively. "I just knew it. I'm smart. I'm a smart kid."

Dubitative Mood:
An epistemic grammatical mood found in some languages, which indicates that the statement is dubious or that the speaker is a suddenly frightened seventeen-year-old girl trying to reassure herself of her own reality as a real person and not just some drug-and-fiction-induced hallucination.

Samantha and War Dog sit on a boulder in the tropical sunshine.

Feel the warmth of the sun on your shoulders and caressing the back of your neck. Smell the salt air, and feel the breeze against your face.

Samantha asks, "What am I missing in the real world right now?"

They're eating a picnic lunch while seated on a boulder, and War Dog says, "The real world is a little overrated." War Dog says, "Don't ask how I found him."

Sam asks, "Found who?"

War Dog says, "Found *whom.*" He says, "I thought you were smart."

War Dog and Samantha are sitting on the warm, rough stone on a volcanic hillside. The boulder sits on the far shore of the lake, with The Orphanage gleaming whitely in the distance. They both gaze at the domes and towers of it across the still waters. Palaces upon palaces, they see.

"Online," War Dog says, "he was calling himself Randy Morning-wood." The Dog gobbles down a slice of *Schwarzwälder kirschtorte.* The cherry filling oozes out the corners of his mouth. Through a mouthful of sweetness he describes some no-name cam site. You needed to buy tokens to stay in the feed. A live cam feed. Extra tokens if War Dog wanted stuff to happen.

Ctrl+Alt+Flashback. There on the computer screen sat a naked man. His arms and neck looked wormy with veins. All his veins were on the outside, like from long-term steroid use. His dingus flopped sideways across one tanned thigh. Here he sat, sprawled on a black vinyl sofa that creaked with his every move. He was so tan even his junk was tanned.

In the scene War Dog typed: *Hey hello.* And hit Enter. The words posted on a chat that ran along one side of the screen.

On screen, the man said, "Hey back. What can I do you for?"

No one else was in the feed. War Dog's words were alone in the chat sidebar. He posted:

Is your name really Randy Morningwood?

On the screen, the man stroked himself. He lifted his legs until the soles of his bare feet bracketed the view of the rest of him. The skin of his soles, yellow, the skin looked cracked and

terrible, his toenails hoary and yellow-brown. The stranger asked, "You want me to go down on myself? Hit me with a few tokens."

War Dog typed:

No, thank you, I don't want to see you go down on yourself, thank you.

The way the man slouched, with his pelvis tilted forward, he thrust his junk front and center. A thick chrome ring, thick as a Rolex watchband, cinched his junk tight. Below that, a pink plastic doohickey jutted out of his old man's hole. The size of a pink cigar, maybe, or a big thumb. Just sticking out a little.

War Dog typed:

No offense, but are you gay?

"You mean this?" the man asked in a gritty microphone voice. He reached down between his legs and tapped the doohickey. "Hit me with some tokens, and I'll answer."

War Dog forked over a couple tokens.

A loud *cha-ching* sound rang out. A tiny light on the end of the pink doohickey lit up bright purple. It blinked neon pink, flashing as this Randy Morningwood squirmed around like he'd been railed by lightning. He slapped one hand over his heart and panted, "Thanks . . ." He squinted at his monitor. "War Dog. You're the best. Daddy loves that."

Morningwood shook off the buzz. "Kid, I'll be whatever floats your boat. I'm just doing this to keep the lights on, okay?"

War Dog typed:

Do you have any children?

The naked man held himself in one hand and slapped his hardness into the palm of his other hand. In his gritty microphone voice he said, "No. I got no kids."

War Dog typed:

Are you sure?

One of the man's hands roved up to his chest and began to tweak his nipple. Both of his nipples were pierced with chrome rings.

The gritty voice asked, "You want me to be your daddy?"

War Dog hit Enter to send a couple tokens.

A loud *cha-ching*. Morningwood squirmed. His eyes crossed, and something fell from his gaping mouth.

War Dog had to look away during that part. He typed:

What was that? The words appeared in the chat sidebar.

The man on camera busied himself, digging one hand between the sofa cushions. He dragged out something white and snugged it back into his mouth. It had been the upper plate of a pair of dentures. He spoke without looking at the camera. "Let Daddy feed you his big meat, baby." His eyes looked at something off camera. He asked, "You want Daddy's love? You want Daddy to love on you?" He continued to stroke himself.

The man on the screen asked, "You think I'm hot? You think Daddy is hot?" Always stroking himself. His gritty voice said, "Tell Daddy how much you love him."

One generation displaying itself naked for the love and approval of another generation.

War Dog typed:

Do you have a daughter named Stephanie?

From Your Practical Guide to Greener Pastures, Sixth Edition, Revised and Updated

A Helpful Hint: Check Out the Message Boards!

Emilee and I had been married almost eleven years when she asked for the divorce. Of our three children, the youngest had just taken the LAP test. All three had shown exceptionally high potential, so it goes without saying that she wanted sole custody.

She knew the score. Those kids had a combined Greener Pastures value estimated to be nine hundred million. Figure the severance on that, and she's talking about shutting me out of a ninety-million-dollar payday.

What's a loving dad to do? I posted on some message boards for Greener Pastures parents. Helpful strangers pushed for me to take Em

on a second honeymoon. To put the kids with relatives and spirit Emilee off to a romantic sky chalet, someplace isolated in the snowy mountains. There was more to it, but that was the basic plan. Not that it would make any difference marriage-wise.

As we made the drive, I never mentioned the kids or the idea that she was trying to rip me off. Me, who'd driven those kids to immersion Portuguese and driven them to the orthodontist.

When we arrive, a maid is hanging fresh towels in the bathroom of the chalet. Em doesn't give her a look until this maid turns around to face us full on. At that, Em says, "What's this happy horseshit?"

At the urging of other Greener Pastures parents, I'd contacted one of those genetic testing outfits. It was Ancestry.com or 23andMe or something. You send them a batch of pictures of yourself, and they search some worldwide database of facial recognition software and find everyone who looks exactly like you.

That's how I'd found Katinka herding goats in some Iron Curtain village. Our deal was that for a half million dollars she'd travel here, me paying all expenses. You see, I'd sent the website photos of Emilee.

Em sees Katinka, and the moment is like looking in a mirror. I don't explain anything, just slip off my belt and whip it around Em's neck, and choke her to death. Where Katinka's from she's seen worse. She stays in-country long enough to pose as Em. She signs child custody over to me, and we divorce, and she's on the next plane home. It's a piece of cake.

The takeaway is this: Don't get greedy. Don't try to pull the rug out from under your spouse. And the message boards for Greener Pastures parents are a godsend. Check them out!

Full Name Withheld Upon Request

Sitting on the boulder, looking across the volcanic lake at the gleaming buildings in the distance, Samantha asks, "What do you think death will be like?"

Stuffing his mouth with cake, War Dog describes the muscle man on the cam show.

On the computer screen, the man lifted his chin. His free hand stroked the bristly, cropped little hairs of his chest and neck. Absently, he asked, "You want Daddy to kiss you?" He asked, "You want Daddy to notice you?" He rubbed together the fingers and thumb of his free hand, a signal.

War Dog hit Enter. The *cha-ching* sounded.

The Morningwood man creaked around on the black vinyl sofa. The pink light in his ass blinked on and off a few times. After the buzz passed, he took off his glasses a moment and mopped tears from his eyes.

This Morningwood person dug deeper between the sofa cushions and brought out a pair of Poindexter eyeglasses. He put them on, bifocals to judge from the way he tilted his face back and looked through the bottom half of each lens. It was clear now that he was looking in a mirror.

War Dog typed:

Are you sure you don't know a Stephanie?

The man squinted and shook his head. He made a fist with his free hand and brought the fist to his mouth. He coughed and coughed. Coughed and coughed. When he finally swallowed and caught his breath, he said, "Sorry. I have a cold." He tapped a finger to one ear. "The cold's got into my fallopian tube."

War Dog typed:

Please, ar you absoluty cetain you dont know a stephanie?

The man stroked himself and said, "Hit me."

War Dog paid him. The *cha-ching*. The pink light. The thrashing and creaking on the vinyl sofa.

As he shook off the buzz, the man said, "Stephany, of course, my sweet baby! Come to Daddy! Daddy loves you. Daddy loves his little slut."

Here it was, watching this on a computer screen, that Stephanie "War Dog" Lefkowitz started to cry.

143

Chuck Palahniuk

From **Your Practical Guide to Greener Pastures, Seventh Edition**
A Cautionary Tale from Allison and Graham W——

We never told Duane. A lot of kids still don't know about Greener Pastures. Most kids don't know. It's like sex education: At what point do you want to open up that can of worms?

Our son, Duane, a friend of his went off to sleepover camp and "died." Duane was wrecked by losing his best friend. Throughout the funeral he wept openly. The "dead" boy's parents looked at us with such pity in their eyes. Our son was in so much pain.

Of course, we could've told Duane the truth. That his friend had gone off to be the next king of whatnot country, but that would be a step down the path to telling Duane everything.

Eventually he'd want to post himself. Kids are curious. Whether or not they actually become full-fledged candidates, most kids want to see what they're worth. The awful truth is that we'd already posted Duane. We'd posted him three times, and he's never met the floor bid. The minimum we'd set. He's a bright kid, he just tests poorly. And after three failed listings, the market consensus is against him.

Honestly, we weren't trying to sell him. We were simply curious, but like they say, curiosity killed the cat. Someday Duane might discover Greener Pastures through the grapevine. He might post himself, but he'll see his auction history and be devastated: first, that we'd posted him without his consent, and second, that nobody had wanted him. We couldn't give Duane away.

It's like that antique appraisal show on public television. People take in treasures they've cherished and cared for, a painting, for example, that's been preserved and passed down to them for generations. Going on that Antiques Roadshow *should be a victory lap, but the appraiser tells them it's not a Rembrandt. The owners find out their treasure is garbage, and they feel angry and foolish. The painting still has sentimental value, but that's all it has. When you put a price on something precious,*

144

it's spoiled. The only difference is that the painting will never find out it's worthless.

Full Names Withheld Upon Request

Sitting on the boulder, Samantha pretends to gaze across the lake. She pretends not to see the tears rolling down War Dog's face. Sam asks, "Don't you miss your real life? I mean, when you're out babysitting people in books?"

War Dog dashes away his tears. "Intervening," he says. "My job is to intervene."

On the computer screen, Randy Morningwood sat, legs spread wide, on his black vinyl sofa. Half the doohickey poked out of his butt like a pink plastic dukey. A bare foot propped on either side of the camera. He reached down and snugged the doohickey deeper inside himself. He snapped his fingers. He curled a couple fingers in a gesture for War Dog to pay up.

On cue, War Dog forked over some tokens. The pink *cha-ching* went off.

Morningwood did his shimmy against the sofa. His gritty voice asked, "So, Steph, you like this fat piece of meat?" He stroked himself. "Steph?" He ground his tanned shoulders into the black vinyl.

A cat walked through the shot, passing between the camera and the cam show hero. The cat gave the camera a meow, and its eyes flashed green-gold. The cat moved along.

Waving after the cat, Morningwood said, "That's Mr. Buddy. Don't mind him."

War Dog typed:

You ver get anyone pregnt? The words popped up in the chat sidebar.

The man yawned. His gritty microphone voice asked, "You want Daddy to get you pregnant?"

From Your Practical Guide to Greener Pastures, Tenth Edition, Revised
FAQ: Doesn't the Family and Familial Love Count for Anything in the New Economy?

Don't be an alarmist. Recognize that there is no new frontier. There is no virgin soil to be tilled. You are the new product. Your offspring are the only crop you can bring to market. The wealthy and powerful need you just as much as you need a payday. Bear in mind that the family has traditionally been among the greatest sources of human unhappiness. Greener Pastures puts your happiness back where it belongs . . . under your own control.

The family is obsolete. The reproductive act serves only to provide a commodity for the market. In the glorious new economy, you're what counts!

Sitting on the boulder in the sunshine, War Dog looks down at his handful of *Schwarzwälder kirschtorte*. He describes how the man on the cam show snapped his fingers. He stroked his hardness while he said, "You wanna see Daddy blow a load? You have to pony up some tokens."

War Dog keyed in some money. More money than he had in the real world. More money than Stephanie would see in a hundred years stocking shelves at Hobby Lobby. More money than the spaces on the tokens field would allow. Then he keyed in a little less money until the amount fit the field. A lifetime's income for most people.

Morningwood, or whoever he was, the man stroked himself close to the camera now. The looming red of him filled the screen. Shining and veined with horrible veins, while his gritty

voice demanded, "Show Daddy how much you love him, Steph. Bring Daddy home with a big payday. Make it rain for Daddy!"

The stranger on camera bucked his hips, faster and faster, into his tight fist.

At his keyboard, War Dog hit Send.

Ctrl+Alt+Climax. Whoever he was, the camera man spazzed and thrashed and clutched his chest, then fell back limp and gasping. An avalanche of clanking money, a thunder of Las Vegas–jackpot-silver-dollar sounds drowned out his bellowing, wordless, hollering moans. His breathing whistled as if his chest were filled with canary birds. Even under his tan, he faded to a dusty pale. His eyelids fluttered for a bit as the pink butt light blinked and the *cha-ching* kept *cha-ching*ing. His hand slipped from his chest and fell across the sofa cushion beside him, and the fingers twitched. His head lolled loose on his neck, and his upper plate slipped out and half his teeth disappeared between the cushions. Soon enough the plastic light went dark. The screen went so still and silent it looked as if the feed had frozen.

From Your Practical Guide to Greener Pastures, Ninth Edition
A Cautionary Tale from Myfanwy M——

It should come as no surprise that drug use follows higher education. Both are based on feel-good chemicals. At first the participation trophies and hugs-for-all of competition. By the upper grades, those kudos piddle out or fail to produce the same intoxicating effect. There are few hugs in high school. The truth is, no one's doling out group hugs and warm fuzzies in the adult world. When the trophies run out, the drug dealer steps into the picture.

War Dog worried his IP address was recorded. He worried this might constitute murder by cryptocurrency. Unsure what to do, he watched and waited.

As the hours ticked by the tanned belly began to swell. The only sound was the video cat, Mr. Buddy, crying over and over. Yowling, the way a baby might cry.

War Dog watched in a vigil over the body. Waiting.

On the computer screen the cat leapt up onto the sofa and leaned into Morningwood's ribs, rubbing its head.

War Dog must've fallen asleep. He blinked awake to the soft sound of pounding from the computer. Then a louder pounding noise came from off camera. A man's voice shouted, *"Was ist das stinken?"* A loud crash crashed and the same voice said, *"Berühren Sie nichts!"* Figures stumbled into the shot, each with his hands cupped over his mouth and nose.

***From* Your Practical Guide to Greener Pastures, Sixth Edition, Revised and Updated**
FAQ: Doesn't Greener Pastures Amount to Chattel Slavery?

On the contrary, what we're offering is the greatest advance in human freedom since the Middle Ages. Since the beginning of history children have been serfs born into bondage to their families. Children are the peasants held in a feudal system that grants them limited rights and freedoms until they reach maturity.

The family unit amounts to a fiefdom. The Civil Rights Movement has completely neglected the autonomy of children.

Henceforth, every child will have the access to a new life. Children can choose their circumstances. Even those who remain with their originating families will find that the presence of Greener Pastures gives them great leverage in negotiating their living conditions.

As they sit on the sun-warmed boulder, War Dog tells Sam, "Let's just say that in real life I owe people a shit-ton of money." He adds, "Like organized crime people." He licks the sticky chocolate cake off his fingertips.

Between the sessions of classroom work, a personal trainer marches Samantha around the jungle trails. War Dog tags along, forever nibbling at a fistful of veal Zsa Zsa Gabor as they trudge the well-worn paths up and down the volcanic slopes. His wallet chain rattling with every step. His boots crunching on the crushed coral surface of the path.

Sam wears the regulation-weight practice crown. In this heat it makes her scalp itch.

The trainer wears a whistle hung on a cord around her neck, and she fingers its chrome as her lips say, "We can't have a chubby Queen Samantha, now can we?"

As Sam pinches the damp front of her sweat suit and pulls it away from her skin, she chides War Dog. "Your pseudo-caveman routine? Your piggishness? If you ask me, it seems a little put-on."

War Dog tosses the uneaten handful of veal. He trots along beside her and the trainer. War Dog farts.

Sam tries a different tack. "Why an Interventionist?"

War Dog chews. He swallows. He seems not to listen to Sam. The Dog is transfigured with joy. An ecstasy of happiness dominates him. He stops.

They stop.

"Dorian, Dorian," War Dog suddenly cries, "before I knew you, acting was the one reality of my life. It was only in the theatre that I lived. I thought that it was all true. I was Rosalind one night and Portia the other. The joy of Beatrice was my joy, and the sorrows of Cordelia were mine also. I believed in everything. The common people who acted with me seemed to me to be godlike. The painted scenes were my world. I knew nothing but shadows, and I thought them real. You came—oh, my beautiful love!—and you freed my soul from prison. You taught me what reality really is. Tonight, for the first time in my life, I saw through the hollowness, the sham, the silliness of the empty pageant in

which I had always played. Tonight, for the first time, I became conscious that the Romeo was hideous, and old, and painted, that the moonlight in the orchard was false, that the scenery was vulgar, and that the words I had to speak were unreal, were not my words, were not what I wanted to say. You had brought me something higher, something of which all art is but a reflection. You had made me understand what love really is. My love! My love! Prince Charming! Prince of life!"

Sample questions from the 2037 Scholastic Aptitude Test:
1. Why are you sometimes sad and unfulfilled?
2. Have people stopped contacting you because you smell bad?
3. Would you be the last one to know if you were losing your mind?
4. Are you so scarred by false starts that you'll never find true love?
5. Does your mom know she raised a sociopath?
6. Why does the algorithm think you want to look at ads for self-adhesive roofing underlayment?
7. Was it something you said?
8. Do you really have free will?
   Please show your work.

Nonplussed, Samantha begins walking again. To burn calories. "So, you're an out-of-work actor slumming?"

War Dog winks.

Here Samantha knows her next line, and turns on War Dog. As naturally as she had known the steps of the gavotte. By intuition. As if she were a character in *The Picture of Dorian Gray*, "Yes," she cries, "you have killed my love. You used to stir my imagination, War Dog. Now you don't even stir my curiosity. You simply produce no effect. I loved you because you were marvel-

ous, because you had genius and intellect, because you realized the dreams of great poets and gave shape and substance to the shadows of art. You have thrown it all away. You are shallow and stupid!"

War Dog glowers at her.

This part is about holding the reader's hand underneath the stream from the faucet while signing the word "water" into the reader's other hand.

You connect the dots.

A low moan breaks from War Dog, and he flings himself at Sam's feet and lies there like a trampled flower. "Dorian, Dorian, don't leave me!" War Dog whispers. "I am so sorry I didn't act well. I was thinking of you all the time. But I will try—indeed, I will try. It came so suddenly across me, my love for you. I think I should never have known it if you had not kissed me—if we had not kissed each other. Kiss me again, my love. Don't go away from me. I couldn't bear it." A fit of passionate sobbing chokes War Dog. He crouches on the jungle path like a wounded thing.

The personal trainer just stares. She fingers her whistle.

"Okay," Sam says. "You're not a *good* actor. But I can see the benefit in this job."

War Dog rises from his crouch. He belches and scratches himself. "What else are you going to do with a degree in Theatrical Arts?"

29

In the limousine on the way to the island's state-of-the-art abortion clinic, Sam sits with her arms crossed, staring daggers at War Dog. "I thought you were supposed to be on my side."

Stifling a yawn, War Dog says, "My job's just to babysit you until the drugs wear off." Impatiently, he recites, "You'll have the abortion. You'll become Queen of England. And you'll live to a ripe old age, unless the drugs wear off first." He'd read this book a million times. Mostly he just reads it now for the food. Screw the birds and flowers.

Mrs. Terry rides in the car with them. Her red-red lips say, "We'll have our abortion, Miss Deel. Then it's back to the salt mines."

Samantha touches her belly lightly. To the baby within her, she whispers, "I'm not having any abortion."

O my sweet! Samantha Deel said inwardly to Frou-Frou, as she listened for what was happening behind. *He's cleared it!* she thought, catching the thud of Gladiator's hooves behind her. There remained only the last ditch, filled with water and five feet wide. Samantha did not even look at the other occupants of the car. Sam felt that she was at her very last reserve of strength; not her neck and shoulders merely were wet, but the sweat was standing in drops on her forehead, her sharp ears, and her breath came in short, sharp gasps. But Sam knew that she had strength left, more than enough for the remaining five hundred yards. It was only from feeling herself nearer the ground and from the peculiar smoothness of her motion that Samantha knew how greatly the

limousine had quickened its pace. They flew over a stone bridge as though not noticing it. They flew over it like a bird, but at the same instant Samantha, to her horror, felt that she had failed to keep up with the story's pace, that she had, she did not know how, made a fearful, unpardonable mistake in trying to thwart the predetermined plot. All at once her position in the car had shifted and she knew that something awful had happened when the roadside flowers flashed by too close. Sam was touching the ground and tumbling across the crushed coral roadbed. She just had time to tuck her legs to her chest. Mrs. Terry had shoved her bodily from the speeding car! Sam fluttered on the ground like a shot bird. The clumsy attack by Mrs. Terry had left her dazed and in a ditch, alone on the muddy, motionless ground, gasping. She struggled all over like a fish, quivered all over and again fell on her side.

A crowd of men, a doctor and his assistant, ran up to Sam. To her misery she felt that she was whole and unhurt. The innocent child she carried, well, that was another matter altogether.

During her period of convalescence at The Orphanage, Sam learns sign language for:

"Ben Birleşik Krallık Hükümdarı Kraliçe Samantha'yım. Sono la regina Samantha, sovrana del Regno Unito."

Samantha Deel's hands learn to lie:

"This is my husband, King Archie, whom I love very much."

Samantha learns the correct fork with which to eat *bacalao al pil pil.*

She rehearses the steps of the *Ballet Royal de la Nuit.*

She perfects her *facultatem sugere in mentulas.*

In the sumptuous bathroom of her apartments at The Orphanage, Sam uses a squeeze bottle to squirt ketchup in her toilet. She lets the butler find the mess and report it to Mrs. Terry. Sam squirts ketchup on a maxi pad and tries to flush it. The toilet clogs and a kowtowing plumber is called to snake the pipes. Samantha does not tell Mrs. Terry or War Dog or the butler or anyone at The Orphanage that her child is still alive.

At the close of her three months' training, she and War Dog board a Bombardier Global 7500. A flight attendant serves them canapés. War Dog selects a radish carved to look like a blossoming rose. He says, "Not to beat a dead horse, but I do love the food in books."

Sam loosens her seatbelt. She's not showing a baby bump yet. First-time mothers with strong core muscles often don't show until the fifth month. Nevertheless, her breasts itch like crazy. She is ravenous. When the flight attendant offers the canapés, Sam takes the entire tray.

War Dog munches away. He asks, "It's none of my business, but are your breasts getting bigger?"

Samantha redirects. "So you're saying this is all a drug trip?"

War Dog flags the flight attendant for a glass of champagne. To Sam he says, "It's more like guided meditation under the effects of primo LSD and crank."

To bring Sam up to speed, War Dog asks, "Do you remember reading a book called *Greener Pastures*?" He explains that she was exposed to a witch's brew of chemicals baked into the book by unscrupulous drug lords. She's not even Sam. Samantha Deel is a character in the book. As the unwitting reader, she/he/whoever is comatose in a hospital ward.

As an Interventionist, War Dog's contract job is to enter the dream and make sure she's not killed. If she dies in the book, she dies in real life.

War Dog says, "If it's any comfort, my name's not War Dog, not in real life," he says. "My real name is Stephanie, but I do

actually work at Hobby Lobby on Lancaster Drive." War Dog wolfs down another fistful of canapés and signals the cabin attendant for more champagne.

Being a freelance Interventionist is tantamount to being a bodyguard in the dream world. The money was shit, but again, the food rocked.

War Dog shakes his shaggy head. "One time I had to babysit this kid who was Harvey in *Captains Courageous.* You know, Rudyard Kipling? I had to tell his folks that Harvey fell off the stupid Portuguese fishing schooner and got bit in half by a sperm whale." War Dog shakes his head sadly. "Poor kid, he died in his coma."

Sam draws back in disbelief. "What's *Captains Courageous?*"

"Some book," says War Dog. "Read it yourself."

Sam eyes the jet's emergency exit hatch. She asks, "What if I pop this hatch and jump out?"

War Dog lowers his chin and gives her a serious look. "Then we both die. I'm in this dream, too." He says, "Just stick to the script. The drugs will wear off, and we'll both go back to our real lives."

And here, the future Queen of England feels the baby inside her begin to stir. She says, "I need the limo to make one stop before I get home. So I can shoplift something from Walgreens."

Samantha Deel was going home to help arrange her own funeral.

***From* Your Practical Guide to Greener Pastures, First Edition, Revised**
A Helpful Hint: Let Your Parents Plan Your Funeral!

Better yet, let your birth parents send you off in style. This makes sense for a couple reasons. First, it gives them an active role to play. Second, it gives them a sense of control. They brought you into this world, so give them the privilege of sending you out! Needless to say, it will be a closed casket or a cremation.

The sooner your originating parents get you buried, the sooner they'll receive their sizable severance fee!

Samantha Deel steps through the door of her family's squalid apartment. Her mother and father reel like zombies in the front hall. Their clothing hangs spiritless on their lank bodies. Their faces stare with vacant eyes. Her father slowly turns toward Sam, his eyes squinting, his brow furrowed with confusion.

His lips stained the telltale green of NyQuil, Mr. Deel's toothless mouth says, "Pumpkin?"

Sam offers the package she's carrying. A peace offering. She's shoplifted an eight-pack of NyQuil.

Tears fill Mr. Deel's eyes. "Girlie-girl," his green-green lips whisper. "You brought your poor mama her medicine." With uncertain steps he comes toward her. His skeleton's hands clamp around the bottles and he tears one free of the rest. This bottle he twists open. He lifts it to his green-green mouth and drinks greedily. The licorice-scented ooze overflows his chin. His tattered plaid shirt hangs unbuttoned, and the cough and cold medication cascades down the boney ribs of his chest and spills onto the littered floor.

The heavy odor of licorice seems to revive Mrs. Deel who has been staring with hollow eyes into a corner at invisible spiders. She looks at Samantha, her daughter, and her green-green lips say, "That nice Mrs. Terry called!" She frowns pathetically. "We're going to miss you, girlie-girl."

Mr. Deel gasps for breath. He hands his wife what's left of the bottle and wipes his mouth lustily with the back of his hand. "Just think of it! Our little girlie-girl is going to be the Queen ah England."

Sam feels herself falling back under the spell of her dismal past. The years of abuse. The filthy diapers. The way she'd been forced to care for her woozy, rummy, NyQuil-besotted parents.

Then, like the magic of an idea, her newfound confidence stiffens her spine. Her hands sign the words, "I'm not going to England! I'm not going to marry a man I don't love! I'm knocked up!"

Her father throws aside the new bottle he's been swilling from. "Like hell you are," his green-green lips say. Seemingly out of nowhere he produces his Weatherby SA-08 twenty-gauge. He levels the barrel straight at her face!

Mr. Deel's green-green lips snarl, "I want that four-point-five million dollars!"

"Four-point-five *hundred* million dollars," Mrs. Deel corrects her husband.

Terror washes over Samantha! Her own parents were going to murder her, right here in the front hall of their squalid apartment!

The words of War Dog come back to her. Sam's hands begin to sign to herself, "This is only a book! This is only a book! This is only a book!" While her feet race to the next room, a blast of the shotgun just misses! A second blast comes, again just missing her head!

As Sam looks around the cluttered sitting room she sees something that takes a moment to register in her mind. An empty wheelchair. Her uncle's wheelchair, empty!

Nearby, her brain-damaged uncle stands, his lips muttering, "Avocado. Avocado. *Avocado.* Avocado. Avocado. Avocado. Avocado. Avocado. Avocado. Avocado. Avocado. Avocado. Avocado. Avocado. *Avocado.* Avocado. Avocado. Avocado. Avocado. Avocado. Avocado. Avocado. Avocado. Avocado. Avocado! Avocado. *Avocado.* Avocado. Avocado. Avocado. Avocado. Avocado. *Avocado!*"

It's clear. The situation is crystal clear. For years her uncle has been feigning paralysis so that Sam would be forced by her own goody-goody-girl nature to bathe him and change his filthy diapers! He towers over her.

His arms are raised above his head. In his hands he holds a

chainsaw, and one hand yanks the pull-cord that brings the saw to screaming life!

His lips screaming, "Avocado!" her uncle advances toward her across the really cramped room.

Her nimble mind comes to the rescue. Quick-thinking Sam sees an open window and throws herself into the void. Her plummet is quick and frightening, but a lush patch of *Brugmansia arborea* cushions her fall. Her and the fetus.

As Samantha Deel climbs to her feet, shaken but unhurt, she sprints away down the impoverished ghetto street, pursued by shotgun blasts, a screaming chainsaw and the lunatic cries, "*Avocado.* Avocado. Avocado. Avocado. Avocado. Avocado. Avocado. Avocado. Avocado. Avocado. Avocado. Avocado. *Avocado.* Avocado. Avocado. Avocado. Avocado. Avocado. Avocado. Avocado. Avocado. Avocado. Avocado. Avocado! Avocado. *Avocado.* Avocado. Avocado. *Avocado.* Avocado. Avocado. Avocado. Avocado. Avocado. Avocado. Avocado. Avocado. Avocado. Avocado. Avocado. *Avocado.* Avocado. Avocado. Avocado. Avocado. Avocado. Avocado. Avocado. Avocado. Avocado. Avocado. Avocado! Avocado. *Avocado.* Avocado. Avocado. Avocado. Avocado. Avocado. Avocado. Avocado. Avocado. Avocado. Avocado. Avocado. Avocado. Avocado! Avocado. *Avocado.* Avocado. Avocado. *Avocado.* Avocado. Avocado. Avocado. Avocado. *Avocado.* Avocado. Avocado. Avocado. Avocado. Avocado. Avocado. Avocado. *Avocado.* Avocado. Avocado. Avocado. Avocado. Avocado. Avocado. Avocado. Avocado. Avocado. Avocado. Avocado! Avocado. *Avocado.* Avocado. Avocado. Avocado. Avocado. Avocado. Avocado. Avocado. Avocado. Avocado. *Avocado.* Avocado. Avocado. Avocado. Avocado. Avocado. Avocado. Avocado. Avocado. Avocado. Avocado. Avocado! Avocado. *Avocado.* Avocado. Avocado. *Avocado.* Avocado. Avocado. Avocado. Avocado. Avocado. Avocado. Avocado. Avocado. *Avocado.* Avocado. Avocado. Avocado.

Avocado. Avocado. Avocado. Avocado. Avocado. Avocado.
Avocado. Avocado! Avocado. *Avocado.* Avocado. Avocado. *Avo-cado.* Avocado. Avocado. Avocado. Avocado. *Avocado.* Avocado.
Avocado. Avocado. Avocado. Avocado. Avocado. *Avocado.* Avo-cado. Avocado. Avocado. Avocado. Avocado. Avocado. Avocado.
Avocado. Avocado. Avocado! Avocado. *Avocado.* Avocado. Avo-cado-Avocado. Avocado. Avocado. Avocado. Avocado. Avocado.
Avocado. Avocado. Avocado. Avocado. Avocado. *Avocado.* Avo-cado. Avocado. Avocado. Avocado. Avocado. Avocado. Avocado.
Avocado. Avocado. Avocado! Avocado. *Avocado.* Avocado. Avo-cado. *Avocado.* Avocado. Avocado. Avocado. Avocado. Avocado.
Avocado. Avocado. Avocado. Avocado. Avocado. Avocado. *Avo-cado.* Avocado. Avocado. Avocado. Avocado. Avocado. Avocado.
Avocado. Avocado. Avocado. Avocado! Avocado. *Avocado.* Avo-cado. Avocado. *Avocado.* Avocado. Avocado. Avocado. Avocado.
Avocado. Avocado. Avocado. Avocado. Avocado. Avocado. Avo-cado. *Avocado.* Avocado. Avocado. Avocado. Avocado. Avocado.
Avocado. Avocado. Avocado. Avocado. Avocado! Avocado. *Avo-cado.* Avocado. Avocado-Avocado. Avocado. Avocado. Avocado.
Avocado. Avocado. Avocado. Avocado. Avocado. Avocado. Avo-cado. *Avocado.* Avocado. Avocado. Avocado. Avocado. Avocado.
Avocado. Avocado. Avocado. Avocado. Avocado! Avocado. *Avo-cado.* Avocado. Avocado. *Avocado.* Avocado. Avocado. Avocado.
Avocado. Avocado. Avocado. Avocado. Avocado. Avocado. Avo-cado. Avocado. *Avocado.* Avocado. Avocado. Avocado. Avocado.
Avocado. Avocado. Avocado. Avocado. Avocado. Avocado! Avo-cado. *Avocado.* Avocado. Avocado. *Avocado.* Avocado. Avocado.
Avocado. Avocado. *Avocado.* Avocado. Avocado. Avocado. Avo-cado. Avocado. Avocado. *Avocado.* Avocado. Avocado. Avocado.
Avocado. Avocado. Avocado. Avocado. Avocado. Avocado. Avo-cado! Avocado. *Avocado.* Avocado. Avocado. Avocado. Avocado.
Avocado. Avocado. Avocado. Avocado. Avocado. Avocado! Avo-cado. *Avocado.* Avocado. Avocado. Avocado. Avocado. Avocado.
Avocado. Avocado. Avocado. Avocado. Avocado! Avocado. *Avo-*

cado. Avocado. Avocado. Avocado. Avocado. Avocado. Avocado. Avocado. Avocado. Avocado. Avocado! Avocado. *Avocado.* Avocado. Avocado. Avocado. Avocado. Avocado. Avocado. Avocado. Avocado. Avocado. Avocado! Avocado. *Avocado.* Avocado. Avocado. Avocado. Avocado. Avocado. Avocado. Avocado. Avocado. Avocado. Avocado! Avocado. *Avocado.* Avocado. Avocado. Avocado. Avocado. Avocado. Avocado. Avocado. Avocado. Avocado. Avocado. Avocado! Avocado. *Avocado.* Avocado. Avocado. Avocado. Avocado. Avocado. Avocado. Avocado. Avocado. Avocado. Avocado. Avocado! Avocado. *Avocado.* Avocado. Avocado. Avocado. Avocado. Avocado. Avocado. Avocado. Avocado. Avocado. Avocado! Avocado. *Avocado.* Avocado. Avocado. Avocado. Avocado. Avocado. Avocado. Avocado. Avocado. Avocado. Avocado! Avocado. *Avocado.* Avocado. Avocado. Avocado. Avocado. Avocado. Avocado. Avocado. Avocado. Avocado. Avocado. Avocado! Avocado. *Avocado.* Avocado. Avocado. Avocado. Avocado. Avocado. Avocado. Avocado. Avocado. Avocado. Avocado! Avocado. *Avocado.* Avocado. Avocado. Avocado. Avocado. Avocado. Avocado. Avocado. Avocado. Avocado. Avocado. Avocado! Avocado. *Avocado.* Avocado. Avocado. Avocado. Avocado. Avocado. Avocado. Avocado. Avocado. Avocado. Avocado! Avocado. *Avocado.* Avocado. Avocado. Avocado. Avocado. Avocado. Avocado. Avocado. Avocado. Avocado. Avocado. Avocado! Avocado. *Avocado.* Avocado. Avocado. Avocado. Avocado. Avocado. Avocado. Avocado. Avocado. Avocado. Avocado! Avocado. *Avocado.* Avocado. Avocado. Avocado. Avocado. Avocado. Avocado. Avocado. Avocado. Avocado. Avocado. Avocado! Avocado. *Avocado.* Avocado. Avocado. Avocado. Avocado. Avocado. Avocado. Avocado. Avocado. Avocado. Avocado. Avocado! Avocado. *Avocado.* Avocado. Avocado. Avocado. Avocado. Avo-

cado. Avocado. Avocado. Avocado. Avocado. Avocado! Avocado. *Avocado.* Avocado. Avocado. Avocado. Avocado. Avocado. Avocado. Avocado. Avocado. Avocado. Avocado! Avocado. *Avocado.* Avocado. Avocado . . ."

According to Marcel Proust, the writer's job is to place the reader in a world so terrible, such an unhappy hellscape of overall chaos, that going back to the real world will feel like escaping to a paradise.

Again, another example of cognitive reframing.

Warning: To repeat, while reading these pages, make a special effort not to touch your nose or mouth. Wash your hands frequently with plenty of soap and warm water. If you experience any feelings of lightheadedness, dizziness, confusion, or heightened sexual arousal, please seek immediate medical attention immediately. This is doubly important if you experience an erection lasting longer than thirty-six (36) hours. Yes, those ED chemicals are also baked into these pages. Neither the author of this book nor its publisher can be held legally liable in the event of any long-term psychosis the reader might develop as a result of consuming this narrative.

Correction: If you do experience a high state of sexual arousal, please seek the author. Thank you.

Picture a glacier, the slow, icy equivalent of a lava flow. However, hot or cold, they both move toward the sea.

30

Alone, expecting a child, Samantha Deel flees to a big, like NBA-big, like Charles Barkley–big mansion in the new Tavistock Woods development. There the smell of smoke greets her nose.

Around a couple turns the street cuts a scorched meadow in half. It pushes through stands of burned-up Christmas trees.

A travel trailer sits in the driveway. Where a house once stood, a fire has magically floated everything down into the basement. The bidet from the second-floor master bathroom. A stainless-steel beverage cooler from the attic media room. The footprint of all the upper floors are superimposed on the floor of the concrete basement, delivered there by the miracles of fire and gravity.

A chimney towers over the mess. Everything reduced to ashes. Ashes and insurance money. The woods slope off in every direction, nothing but brittle and blackened trees. A little ways from the house a disk of grey concrete sits beside a hole in the scorched lawn. A noxious, septic reek wafts out of the hole.

Samantha goes to the travel trailer and knocks.

Before he kissed her in Paris, Garson told her that his parents had used their severance fee to pay cash for an immense mansion in Tavistock Woods. He'd called it a hillbilly Barbie Dream House, and he vowed to take revenge on his scofflaw, soused father. This he said, ironically, even as he swilled his seventh gin martini and plotted in his mind to stealth Samantha! Thus making her ineligible to be a fitting candidate for the fiendish Greener Pastures.

Even now, Sam can still see his lean, handsome face panting over her.

Hit Ctrl+Alt+Best+Intentions.

At the door of the travel trailer, Samantha Deel knocks a second time.

When the flimsy door opens, it takes Sam a beat to see what Momma Stavros is holding. She holds it in both hands, arms straight out in front of her. It's a gun. To be exact, it's a Walther PPQ 45. Heavy enough to absorb its own recoil, yet small enough for fragile lady hands. With excellent stopping power, the gun feeds off a double-stack, twelve-round magazine.

Sam throws up her hands in terror.

Momma Stavros stands in the doorway of the trailer. She backs a step inside. She wears a black dress with her feet in black Pucci slingbacks. Her face draped with a black veil, her veiled lips demand, "Are you here from Greener Pastures?"

Sam shakes her head vigorously.

Momma Stavros waves her inside.

Hands still raised, Sam enters and sits at the built-in dinette table.

Tears well up in her eyes, but Momma Stavros blinks them away. Her lips say, "I'm going to my husband's funeral today." She steps to the tiny fridge and opens it to show boxes of Chinese takeout and a few cans of beer. Her lips ask, "Sam, would you like anything?"

Sam shakes her head.

In this next moment Mrs. Stavros seems spent. She crosses her arms, and her thin hands take on a life of their own, crawling over her like restless spiders or crabs, blue veined and terrible,

but with pink manicured fingernails. It takes the suffering woman a long moment before she can tell her story.

Momma Stavros's eyebrows look like stitches of thread. Black thread, as if a wound has been closed. To Sam, the poor woman's lips look like rose petals, but ones that have fallen off a bouquet and dried on the floor, and if you so much as touched them, her lips would crumble into pink dust.

Mrs. Stavros quickly guzzles a beer and crushes the metal can in her manicured grip, an action that betrays a hidden rage. Her lips say, "Samantha? When you sign your married name, your signature is never as beautiful as the maiden name you learned to write while growing up." Women never like to admit that, she says. "All your married life, your hand hates signing anything. Your hand fights this constant betrayal of the original you." Her voice trails off bitterly.

Sam's hands mime drinking. Her hands sign the words, "Do you have any milk?" She can feel the fetus leaching calcium from her bones.

Mrs. Stavros takes a plastic jug from the little fridge. She pours a glass and sets it on the table before Sam.

Sam Deel gives it a sniff but drinks some anyways. Her mouth vomits the whiteness all over the dinette. The milk has gone sour. Chunky sour.

"Sorry," say Momma Stavros's lips. "I forget." She explains that to maintain a septic tank you need to pour a gallon of spoiled milk down the toilet every couple of months.

Staring out the window in nostalgic reflection, Mrs. Stavros says, "Lonnie made it his habit to stash small bottles of Hennessy." In back of the folded towels in the bathroom, she says, for example. Behind books on a shelf. "And when I found one I'd flush it down the commode, too." She shrugs off the memory. "It's okay.

It's not going into the ocean or anything. Out here in the sticks, it's not going any farther than the septic tank."

She described moving out here after Garson's faked funeral. To this, the only house in a new development. Their dream house, bought with their severance money from Greener Pastures.

"Garson wasn't dead a week before he called his father," Momma Stavros says. "Then the agents of Greener Pastures showed up." It was always a pair of thugs, nicely dressed in tailored uniforms, looking to all the world like Secret Service agents. On their first visit they'd caught Mr. Stavros as he answered the door. They clipped off his finger and departed with it while Garson was still on the phone to him.

"I think he just wanted to hear his father's scream," says Momma Stavros.

As per the No-Contact Clause, each communication with an originating parent resulted in the removal of a finger from Garson's dad.

"We bought this," say the lips of Momma Stavros, lifting the handgun for a moment, then placing it on the countertop of the trailer's tiny kitchen.

The lipsticked lips of Mrs. Stavros say, "One evening, Lonnie's phone started to ring, and a car pulled up, and we knew it was Garson calling, and his thugs were waiting for us to pick up."

They'd hit the panic button, Mr. and Mrs. Stavros had. Steel shutters had rolled down over the doors and windows. It was a siege situation. This amounted to a fifth violation, and the goons were there to execute Mr. Stavros. The goons had walked around the perimeter of the house, shouting their demands through a bullhorn. Mr. and Mrs. Stavros had hidden inside. In time, the phone stopped ringing. The shouting stopped. Before long Momma Stavros had smelled smoke.

From a top-floor window, they could see a wall of smoke moving up the street. Flames crowned in the scrubby trees. The grass was tall and dry. Fire season. The goons were trying to flush them out!

How the smoke detectors had whaled! (stet) The house was filled with live ammo, and the roof was catching fire. Lonnie's car exploded where it was parked in the driveway. A fireball went up as the propane tank on the barbeque exploded.

The thugs had set the fire, and both of Garson's parents had faced the surge of flames that blew out of the barrens and swept across their lawn.

Momma Stavros gives Sam a look. Her lips say, "Don't judge me, okay? When you feel death at your back, you'll climb into anything."

Mr. and Mrs. Stavros had bolted from the house and sprinted across the yard. He'd knelt to grab something and strain at it. She'd followed. What he struggled to lift was a concrete disk. She'd knelt beside him and grabbed the two handles he was holding, and together they'd slipped the concrete to one side.

A smell had struck them. Something worse than the smoke. Worse than death. A round hole opened before them, a perfect circle in their front lawn. Even as the heat scorched their hair, the smell that wafted out from this dark hole made them both turn away, gagging. Below them yawned a concrete room with a black glimmer at the bottom.

"Thank our lucky stars the house was so new," say the veiled lips. Otherwise, that big concrete room might've been filled to the ceiling.

As the firestorm had spun a tornado around them, Lonnie Stavros had given his wife one look and lowered himself, feet first, into the stinking hole of their septic tank. His wife, Cindi, felt her Jil Sander blazer begin to kindle. Her diamond wristwatch felt like a white-hot branding iron, and she'd followed suit. For a long moment she'd gripped the concrete rim of the hole, gasping a few last breaths from the sweet world. Only when her arms could no longer hold herself suspended between this world and the next, she felt her fingers slip, and dropped to land next to her husband.

As it was, the muck stood no deeper than their knees.

Sick from the stench, she'd bent double and vomited. She retched until her stomach was empty, and this new stink of acid and bile thickened the smell of smoke and sour milk to the point Mr. Stavros heaved up.

Sunk in their own filth, their feet had slid against a foul, thick layer of slime on the floor. Any wrong move, and one or the other would tumble to land waist deep—or worse—in the mess. Their own unresolved mess.

Just to stay upright, they'd been forced to hold each other. With dirty hands they'd clutched one another more tightly than they had since their wedding night. Each stabilized yet repelled by the other. Each sickened by the unclean reek of the other and the sticky touch of each other's soiled hands.

While the fire raged above. Their dream house had deflated, settling, evaporating in puffs of sparks. While the disaster exhausted itself, they surveyed their new world. The round port overhead was out of their reach, but it had cast a smoky, faint tunnel of light down upon them. A spotlight.

The dim light glinted off little bottles floating around their knees. Here were all the tiny bottles of Hennessy. The ones Momma Stavros had flushed down the toilet to deter her husband's secret boozing.

What light fell on them, it was murky with smoke and the wavering stink lines of rising gas.

They'd been cast down.

In the travel trailer, as Momma Stavros tells this, Sam stares back, bug eyed. She chokes back rising nausea.

Mired in the accumulated corruption of their lives, Momma Stavros had plucked a bottle of Hennessy and drunk it. Trapped there together, they'd guzzled Hennessy to escape the reality of their senseless lifelong quest for money and material possessions. As the smoke lifted and the stink drifted up and out the hatch, their moods improved. Each was the only source of warmth the other had.

They'd no way to escape. The opening was too far beyond their reach. But they were alive for this moment and neither was alone to face what they'd always hoped to be rid of.

It was possible that Lonnie could lift her, and she would climb out and go for help. But neither trusted the other not to slide shut the concrete lid and leave them to drink in total darkness, to stumble in the ooze and sit down, and to abandon all hope, eventually, and fall asleep. To drown in the thick, watery blackness.

They'd been grooming Garson since he'd been born. Chess Camp. Immersion Navajo. In the tiny travel trailer, Momma Stavros stares at Sam. Sam still seated at the little dinette table. The black-veiled lips ask, "Do you know what the Lifetime Achievement Potential test is? Every child takes it in second grade, so you might not remember . . ." Her lips say, "Maybe they called it the LAP test, but it determines the impact you're most likely to make in the world."

Samantha ransacks her memory. The Lifetime Achievement Potential test.

Mrs. Stavros smiles with pride. "Do you know what it predicted about Garson? My Garson?" She tosses her chin, beaming. "The test showed an eighty-nine percent probability our Garson would create the cure for most common forms of cancer . . ." Eyes closed, she glows with pride.

But instead of allowing Garson to cure cancer, they'd bullied him into going to The Orphanage and being trained to become a future Pope!

In the unfinished past, Lonnie and Cindi Stavros had stood hugging each other in the collected filth of their lives, steeped in the waste they'd made of their world, still hoping someone would come to the rescue. Some miracle would deliver them.

Eventually the two men in tailored uniforms had appeared, to stand at the brink of the cesspit. Two dark angels outlined

against the smoky sky. The agents of Greener Pastures, they'd offered Mr. Stavros a hand up, and promised to send someone for his wife.

The moment they'd raised him back into the sunlight of the sweet world, they'd put a gun to his head and shot him like a dog.

Before they'd taken their leave, they'd rescued Momma Stavros from the mire and left her to grieve over the body of her husband.

As Momma Stavros adjusts the black veil on her head and prepares to go to the funeral, Samantha's hands sign the words, "Can I borrow that?" She gestures toward the gun on the countertop.

The widow shrugs her black-clad shoulders. Listlessly.

Toting the small, powerful gun, Samantha makes her way back to her family's tawdry apartment. The front door is exploded to bits by shotgun blasts and reckless swings of a chainsaw. In the front hall, she finds a pathetic tableau. Her parents and her uncle sprawl on the littered floor, their faces stained green. Empty bottles of NyQuil lie about. All three of their toothless mouths hang open and snoring.

Silently Sam tiptoes closer. She carefully, silently lifts the shotgun from her father's sleeping hands. Holding her breath, she likewise lays claim to the chainsaw her uncle holds. Lastly, Samantha Deel steals what's left of a stale loaf of French bread from her mother's unconscious grip.

Only then does Sam point the handgun at the trio. She kicks her father's leg, hard. With her free hand, she signs the words, "Wake up!"

Again, louder, she signs, "WAKE UP, YOU BASTARDS!"

Roused by the loud sign language, her father's eyes blink open.

Sam's fingers sign again. This time, they sign by pulling the trigger. A warning shot that slams into the stained wall, exploding a fountain of plaster dust near her uncle's head.

All three of her abusers jolt fully awake. They leap to their feet. Their hands grab for weapons no longer within reach. Their eyes narrow in hatred.

Her mother's green-green lips demand, "Give me the gun, Miss Girlie-girl."

Sam's lithe frame trembles with fear until she recalls the courage of Harvey Cheyne Jr. in *Captains Courageous*. At War Dog's urging, she'd read the inspiring nineteenth-century bildungsroman while on the jet coming home. The way it depicted a young silly boy finding his sea legs and self-confidence, and, well, the book now fills Sam with a newfound boldness.

31

In the stained front hall, seeing his chance, her disgusting, clearly not-crippled uncle leaps at Sam.

She shoots.

The bullet enters him just as the bullet had entered Frou-Frou's head. The revolting pervert catches his comeuppance square in the forehead. His filthy mind bursts out the back of his skull and adds its heinous graffiti to the stained everything of their lives. Like a horse, his dying body flutters on the floor like a shot bird. Like Vronsky had kicked his horse, Sam kicks the dead man in the belly.

Like Sam Spade, Samantha Deel levels the smoking barrel of the gun on her parents. Her free hand says, "Spill the tea, bitches!"

Her mother recoils from the corpse beside her. Her green lips smile and ask, "Girlie-girl, you wouldn't kill your poor mama, would you?"

Sam cocks the trigger.

Her father reaches both hands toward her, palms up, his lips beseeching. "Everything we done, we done for you, girlie-girl . . ."

Her mama lip-synchs, "We only tormented y'all so you'd jump at the first chance to go off and be the Queen of England. We worked hard all your life to make you wanna leave home!"

Sam's papa mimes his love. "Your mama tells no lie, girlie-girl. We saw you was special. Look at us." He gestures mournfully at their shattered, NyQuil-drenched abode. "We're a sinking ship. When you was tiny and the Greener Pastures folks told us you showed promise, we pledged our lives to making you miserable."

It was a system.

Okay, it was a severly fuked-up system, buut a systm. (stet all)

The Lifetime Achievement Potential test. LAP for short. The test to which Momma Stavros had referred.

Now Sam feels certain her divine muse is with her, her genie, her *idios daemon*. Embraced by her mentoring spirit, Samantha Leaux Deel sights down the barrel of her gun and her free hand demands, "What did the test show was my destiny?"

As she looks on, her parents are transformed. Her mother sheds that walleyed-hillbilly, gasoline-huffer's stoop. In the blink of an eye her hootenanny mannerisms fall away, she and Sam's father straighten their spines and take on an aristocratic flair. For his part, her father squares his shoulders and wipes the remaining NyQuil from his square-jawed, newly handsome face. With that, they become elegant and wise. He takes his wife's slim fingers and kisses them as might a royal consort.

Her mother speaks first. Her lips say, "Beloved daughter." In dulcet tones without a trace of irritating patois, Mrs. Deel announces, "You have passed a great test!"

Tears of joy spring to her father's eyes as his lips add, "Please forgive us for ever doubting you." Smiling kindly at the gun, he explains that the LAP test had shown Sam held great promise. They'd so hoped she'd fulfill that promise, but they knew in their hearts that her spirit had yet to be tested.

"We only played along with Greener Pastures," say her mother's lips.

"We had to know if you'd be tempted to forego your gifts," says her father. His lips add, "By eschewing the temptations of assured success as the future Queen of England, you've proved yourself worthy of your eternal spirit guides."

Buried in his grave in O'ahu Cemetery in Honolulu, Joseph Campbell smiles.

With that, both of Sam's parents are sobbing with joy.

They'd only been pretending to sell her into human bondage! Like Cinderella she'd been tested by the trial of cleaning the naked body of her pretend-crippled uncle. They'd denied her singing lessons so she'd become stronger. Even by destroying her hearing with baby aspirin, Samantha had followed her gut. She'd placed herself into the same fortress of silence that had nurtured the talents of Thomas Edison and Helen Keller.

Beaming, her mother's lips say, "Our cherished angel!"

Both parents open their arms.

Unable to hold back her heart, Sam drops the gun. She throws herself into their embrace. The three of them, at long last a happy family. No longer like something terrible out of Tolstoy's imagination. Their hearts heave together. Four hearts in total, because now the teeny heart already beats in the young girl's womb.

The world is a wonderful place.

¡El mundo es un lugar maravilloso!

Le monde est un endroit merveilleux!

Sasāra ika śānadāra jag'hā hai!

Maailma on ihana paikka!

Thế giới là một nơi tuyệt vời!

Is áit iontach é an domhan!

Il mondo è un posto meraviglioso!

Umhlaba uyindawo enhle!

دنیای جای شگفت انگیزی است!

Mae'r byd yn lle bendigedig!

Die Welt ist ein wunderbarer Ort!

Even there, restored to the bosom of her joyous family, an idea is burning a hole in her pocket. With one free hand, Sam asks, "But what did the Lifetime Achievement Potential test predict as my great destiny?"

In response, her mother's lips whisper, "You are fated to destroy the evil empire of Greener Pastures!"

32

Sam's mission is clear to her. She dries her tears and bids her family goodbye. Her destiny awaits. Only one agent of the evil empire is within her reach, and Sam will start there.

Quickly she sorts through her meager wardrobe and selects a black dress. She adorns her head with a black veil that masks her resolute young visage. Her lips firmly set. Her eyes steely. She stashes the Walther PPQ 45 in a black patent-leather handbag and sets off for the church.

You see, a good teller is more a radio or a television. A good teller doesn't invent stories any more than your phone does. Or a customized steamroller. You see, a good storyteller is attuned. Stories fill the air we breathe.

A good spinner simply picks the best stories out of that air.

The church had finally rebuilt their stained-glass window. Picture a garden of red and yellow, tulips and daffodils, blue and lavender, cornflowers and irises, orange and pink, poppies and roses. Above these spreads an eternally blue sky.

Imagine such optimism!

Below this phony garden lies the casket of Lonnie Stavros. Beloved husband and father.

Seated in attendance among the many bereaved is Mrs. Terry. Mrs. Doom herself wears her tailored black suit. Her pointed witch's shoes. Her red-red lips behind a black veil. The truth is,

this town is wrung dry of promising candidates. In another week Mrs. Terry will slip off to another high school. In attendance is Mrs. Stavros, who once spread her legs to make peace.

The circus was folding its tent.

It's a system.

Esmond Jensen's mother stands in line to pass the coffin, as do the parents of Anne Lewis-Kennedy. Sam stands to one side, the gun hidden in the folds of her skirt.

The organ plays. The choir sings.

This sight is almost Sam's undoing. To see the choir sing, yet not to hear them. To see their joyous, rapt faces. It brings to mind all she has lost by going deaf. The entire opportunity cost of destroying her own hearing. She'll never again feel the incredible ecstasy of her own voice. She'll never know the power of the one talent that sustained her throughout her life. That joy is forever lost to her.

. . . One autumn night, five years before, they had been walking down the street when the leaves were falling, and they came to a place where there were no trees and the sidewalk was white with moonlight. They stopped here and turned toward each other. Now it was a cool night with that mysterious excitement in it that comes at the two changes of the year. The quiet lights in the houses were humming out into the darkness and there was a stir and bustle among the stars. Out of the corner of his eye Gatsby saw that the blocks of the sidewalks really formed a ladder and mounted to a secret place above the trees—he could climb to it, if he climbed alone, and once there he could suck on the pap of life, gulp down the incomparable milk of wonder.

His heart beat faster as Daisy's white face came up to his own. He knew that when he kissed this girl, and forever wed his unutterable visions to her perishable breath, his mind would never

romp again like the mind of God. So he waited, listening for a moment longer to the tuning fork that had been struck upon a star. Then he kissed her. At his lips' touch she blossomed for him like a flower and the incarnation was complete.

"Keep your hands off the lever," snapped the elevator boy.

"I beg your pardon," said Mr. McKee with dignity, "I didn't know I was touching it."

That, as so beautifully demonstrated by Francis Scott Fitzgerald, is shock induction.

Unlike Jay Gatsby, Samantha Deel would live beyond her early infatuation. She could weep over her lost joy, then live on to fulfill a dream she'd never dared to recognize. A dream, the secret hidden her, only now revealed to her. This unrecognized dream had sustained her through the worst.

Surrounded by the thundering silence of the invisible organ music and the song of the choir, Samantha Deel lifts the gun from her skirt. She takes aim down the barrel. A close-range bullseye, aimed directly at the veiled head of Mrs. Terry.

Hit Ctrl+Alt+Inevitable. The sanctuary doors crash open, and the crowd turns to see a ragged figure stagger in. This stumbling scarecrow flaps his arms, wearing the tatters of ragged clothing. Barefoot, his neck circled with vivid, red noose burns, he lurches down the center aisle. The young man's lips scream, "Mrs. Terry is the devil!"

Here is Garson Stavros himself, back from the dead. Twice.

Too many mourners stand up for a better look. They block a straight shot at Mrs. Terry. Samantha sidesteps for a better angle.

The walking corpse of Garson staggers down the church aisle.

His corpse lips shout, "Mrs. Terry is the frontman for an evil corporation that provides staffing for the entire corrupt world!"

Ragged and dehydrated, he stumbles deeper into the church, shouting, "It's in the Bible, Matthew 4:8–9." Shouting, *"The devil took him to a very high mountain and showed him all the kingdoms of the world and their splendor. 'All this I will give you,' the devil said, 'if you will bow down and worship me' . . ."*

Crazed and bug-eyed, Garson Stavros's lips scream, "Greener Pastures is robbing our children of their souls and robbing mankind of the gifts and talents that will save the planet!"

Sam, unnoticed, angles for a new shot. Too many gawkers stand in the way.

At the pulpit now, Garson's lips sputter, "Samantha will rise to restore the future of humanity!"

Here Mrs. Terry signals to her goon squad. The agents, perhaps the same ones who executed Mr. Stavros, these agents close in to end this show.

Left with no choice, Garson staggers backward until he strikes the wall beneath the altar window. There, as Samantha had done not so very long ago, Garson hauls himself up to the windowsill. As hands try to grab him, this flailing, barefoot apparition in tattered clothes, he jabs an elbow to smash out a glass tulip in the window and use the hole as a handhold. He stomps a bare heel to bust out a glass daffodil for a foothold, and he's climbing. Supported only by thin stained glass and thinner threads of lead, young Garson climbs a makeshift ladder to escape the hands grabbing at him from below.

He breaks out colored-glass peonies and roses as he ascends toward the blue-blue sky. His feet bare and bleeding, he kicks. His bare fists hammer. And doing so Garson Stavros vanquishes this garden of fake lilies and doves.

Mrs. Terry lifts her phone and begins to record the scene. So Garson will look insane. So no one will ever believe his ranting about the shadowy empire of Greener Pastures. So the operation

can move on to a new community and harvest the souls of its most gifted.

Everyone lifts their phones. As so many cameras record, Garson tries to crawl out through a hole he's busted in the sky. It's then the whole illusion gives way. The bulk of stained-glass Heaven and Earth falls away. The black spiderweb that had held all creation in place, the thin strips of lead cinch around the young man's neck. A tangled knot of black strands closes tight around his neck so that he does his gallows dance, arms and legs punching and kicking until all of creation showers down in rainbow fragments upon the casket of his dead father.

His body, dangling in air. So much dead weight, suspended from the snare of wadded metal. His face, dark and horrible, is recorded by so many cameras; his body goes limp, twisting at the end of a noose, slowly twisting until he comes to face the multitude.

Angel lust there to make everyone blush. The divine made all too human.

The shadow of this dead man falls over the people watching from below.

The show is complete.

We straggled down quickly through the rain to the cars. Owl-Eyes spoke to me by the gate.

"I couldn't get to the house," he remarked.

"Neither could anybody else."

"Go on!" He started. "Why, my God! They used to go there by the hundreds."

He took off his glasses and wiped them again, outside and in.

"The poor son of a bitch," he said.

33

Author's Note: All stories are told after the fact. Years ago, I made an appearance at Grauman's Egyptian Theatre in Hollywood, after which a small group of middle-aged people approached me. They beamed with pride as they told me that they were billionaires. Filled with a passion for literature, these strangers told me how they were spending a small fraction of their fortunes to create a growing website. They wanted to spread their love of books so much that they'd even customized the roller part of a steamroller. A huge, heavy machine used to flatten everything in its path. The roller had been customized with printing plates and a system to continuously ink them. As the machine rolled the streets, it would print copies of famous works of fiction in its wake. And no, I am not inventing this. If only I were. These billionaires told me that their life's dream was to make all literature available to all people at no cost. Regardless of copyright or even the smallest payment to the authors, their website would improve the world by making all works of fiction as worthless as sand.

They waited for me to thank them.

34

As the crowd shrieks and continues to record the dead body, Sam steps up beside Mrs. Terry and sticks the barrel of the gun in her ribs.

From **Your Practical Guide to Greener Pastures, Fifth Edition**
FAQ: What's Next for Greener Pastures?

In the near future, even mediocre students will strive for academic honors. Such awards will garner them higher online bids and thus a greater severance fee for their originating parents. Not to mention a greater status and destiny for themselves!

Lesser students might be adopted by enterprising families or individuals who hope to provide a few years of rigorous schooling and drilling that will turn those lackluster candidates into scholars and sportsmen who can eventually bring a top price and hefty severance fee to the investor(s).
Buy low, sell high. Yes, the wily parents will be "flipping" kids!

Increasingly, Greener Pastures intends to down-market to provide lesser quality adoptees to the upper-middle-class households that can't afford our current stellar candidates. Children born into families at all socioeconomic levels will study rigorously for fear of losing their parents' love to a more qualified adoptee attained through the Greener Pastures marketplace.

And while our organization stands to turn a tidy profit, it's society at large that will reap the true rewards!

Chuck Palahniuk

A Dassault Falcon 10X private jet carries Sam Deel and her hostage back toward Honeymoon Island.

As the nervous flight attendant serves them a delicious stream of *amuses-bouche en croûte*, Sam keeps her gun trained on Mrs. Terry's forehead.

Sam presses on. "What can you tell me about the Lifetime Achievement Potential test?"

Mrs. Terry laughs. Likely loopy with fear, she says, "I can tell you that Esmond Jensen showed a ninety-four percent likelihood he'd resolve global warming. And that Anne Lewis-Kennedy was all set to eradicate AIDS . . . and that Myfanwy Mulvaney demonstrated a . . ." Here she takes a sip of champagne from a tall flute. "The test showed that Myfanwy Mulvaney had a ninety-three percent likelihood of resolving systemic racism."

The world had lost all of this potential progress.

Samantha wants to know something. It's no longer enough to pass a test, now she wants to know the things her teacher didn't want to teach. All the secrets. She asks, "A test can determine all that?"

Mrs. Terry begins to explain something about likely outcomes and testing matrices and genetic presuppositions, but stops herself. She starts down a new avenue, explaining the science of intuition-allowanced probability prediction, but pulls herself up short. "It's a ninety-eight percent certainty," she shrugs. It's too much to tackle at the point of a gun.

A kind of game-show elation begins to well up in Sam. She asks, "Can you take me to meet the leader of Greener Pastures?"

Mrs. Terry's red-red lips say, "Picture yourself in a garden. You walk into a garden along a gravel pathway. A narrow pathway. Behold the dangling bell-shaped flowers of *Brugmansia arborea*, also known as angel's trumpet. Put your nose to a blossom and breathe in the sweet-smelling scent—"

Sam's free hand interrupts, signing the words, "One more lip movement, and I'll blast your fucking head off!!!!"

Singing and Signing. Glaciers and lava flows. They're both kind of the same deal.

In short:

$$\mathbf{F}=GmMr2$$

What hypnotists called anchoring.

35

Mrs. Terry drives them in a limousine. Through the rolling landscape of Honeymoon Island, through forests of tree ferns and steaming swamps pink with flamingoes. Past ancient statues crusted with moss, and roaring waterfalls. They ride in the car back up the slopes of the dead volcano and across the cinder-cone islands that dot the caldera lake. Back toward The Orphanage. In the leather-smelling car, Sam's hand asks, "Why did you give up your singing career?"

Not a minute or a mile later, without a glance down or a flickering corner of her mouth that says otherwise, Mrs. Terry says, "You're young." Her lips say, "But someday you'll be too old to remember what you can't remember. You'll be too old to remember what you can't remember you can't remember." Hers is the voice of someone who doesn't exist in a world of gritty public transportation or crowded supermarkets. Her every stitch and hair in place, she says, "We handle the staffing needs for the entire world. I'll always be cared for."

A view opens between rocks and trees. The sky and lake, two shades of bright blue, meet along a straight, flat horizon.

At this juncture the car rolls up to the many white mansions of The Orphanage. Fountains sparkle, and peacocks strut across the broad stone steps. There, a uniformed guard steps to one side and salutes. The little butler that Sam already knows, wearing the usual dark suit, stands at the bottom step and opens her door. The butler with the child's body and the man's head, his lips say, "Miss Deel, thank you for coming back to join us."

At the top of the front steps the butler opens the door and waves Sam inside. A foyer, but nothing she hasn't seen in history books. The usual carved-stone everything: statues, a stairway winding down from a distant upper floor. Their footsteps echo across polished stone, slippery white as an ice-skating rink. Pieces of furniture crop up, set as far apart as items in a museum, polished wood. Tapestry. The usual throne-room stuff, nothing that looks sat on, ever. Sam and the little butler enter a room as big as the inside of a church, after that another room. A suite as big as a shopping mall, complete with planter boxes and full-sized palm trees that don't come close to reaching the high ceiling. The butler matches Sam's pace or she matches his. They are each other's shadow. His lips ask, "If you please, Miss Deel, your gun?"

Sam's kept the gun concealed in her bag. Here she surrenders it, trading the gun for a bigger idea: Why kill just the leader when she might be able to kill the hive?

The way thoughts just bubble to the surface in your mind.

Without breaking his stride, the butler accepts the pistol. They pass under an archway, and into a vast room of billowing curtains and carved everything. "Please." The butler nods toward a chair big enough for three people. "Would you have a seat?"

Sam sits.

The butler clasps his hands together behind his back. "How are you liking your senior year in school?" his lips ask. He looks older than Sam would guess. The grey streaks each side of his hair. The ligaments show under the skin of his neck, but he displays the same hologram detachment as Mrs. Terry, something perfected by a team of artists and inserted here by special-effects magic.

Sam's hands say, "School is school."

Still standing, the butler frowns. "Already disillusioned?" He squats down in front of Sam. Dropping low to meet her eye to

eye. "Miss Deel," his lips say, holding her gaze. "What would you say if I assured you that school is simply a holding pen?"

His lips demand, "What does school offer? The same assembly-line lessons about *The Catcher in the Rye* taught to every kid? Frankly, what is the point?" With a sneer of disgust, his lips say, "Why not take drugs? Why not check out?"

Really, Sam doesn't want drugs. No drug has ever gotten her as high as a perfect test score. A brilliant essay awarded with extra honors, or a chance to present her work at a conference where she could debate head to head with the reigning geek royalty from other schools. As walking brain trusts, they taught each other more than their teachers ever could. Left unsaid is the dismal truth that if their teachers were exceptional, they'd not be mired in public classrooms bludgeoning the idiots with long division.

The butler's lips say, "You, Miss Deel, are gifted beyond the crude methods for measuring human intelligence."

That sort of acknowledgment, that's Sam's Roxicodone and tequila. An embargoed truth the public school system is forbidden to admit to her: Her worth.

Schools save their praise for the slow learners. Remedial kids get the resources, the small class sizes, and one-on-one assistance. The smart kids get *The Catcher in the Rye* and a diploma after wasting a few years in brainless boredom.

The butler checks his wristwatch. He presses a button near his elbow on a side table.

"I remember your terror," he continues. "At seventeen, you're looking at the greatest challenges of your life . . ."

A uniformed maid enters, carrying a tray.

The little butler isn't distracted. "At your age you're painfully aware that you have some ten years to snag a college education, from a renowned university. You must bond with a lifetime mate. Launch a successful career. Establish a decent home, and begin to produce offspring." His lips pause as if to let the impossible challenge crush Sam fully. "The fear is overwhelming."

The maid offers the tray, but he waves it away, his lips saying, "It's no wonder young people succumb to drugs and promiscuity."

The maid offers the tray to Samantha. Little sandwiches fringed with lettuce. Paper-thin slices of meat she can't recognize, between triangles of bread she's never heard of. It's the type of crunchy bread that tears up your gums until whatever you're eating tastes like your own blood. Sam accepts a napkin and places it across one knee, then balances a stack of tiny sandwiches there. Her hands say, "I love the food in books."

She's eating for two now.

"Always hungry at your age," says the butler. "I recall that. But hungry for so much more than food. At thirteen years old, I was sick of coming home to an empty house. I was sick of microwave snacks and video games alone. I wanted a real security and a tangible sense of belonging . . ." His lips continue, "They scout athletes as young as grade school, why shouldn't they scout scholars that young or even younger?"

As she's chewing, Sam's hands ask, "You're not a butler, are you?"

She swallows. Her hands say, "You're so young to be the leader of the whole world." Her hands add, "And so handsome."

He smiles. It seems that flattery is his weakness as well. "At thirteen," say his lips, "I created a new system in which smart children could choose their own destiny." His focus drifts as he recalls, "In the eighties, the suicide rate for teens tripled. Tripled! Those dead kids are now running the world."

He sets the gun on the maid's tray, and the maid carries it away.

As an adolescent, his business model attracted customers, candidates, and investors. Before the internet, the auctions had taken place by telephone, just as they did at Sotheby's and Christie's. The man shakes his head as if dumbfounded by the memory of his own chutzpah. Recalling a kid who had nothing to lose and took every chance.

Now with grey in his hair, he sighs. "Sooner than you think, Samantha, you'll reach an age when you take down your mirrors and start to hang art." He gestures to the paintings and sculpture. "When you can't remember the title of a Jane Wyman film . . . only it's actually everything you can't recall."

And he proceeds to tell Sam everything.

Those numbers on your microwave? Every reheated cup of coffee is counting down the seconds of your life.

The butler isn't a butler. The butler is The Director of Greener Pastures. In The Orphanage, he tours Sam through the polished stone riches of the world.

Intelligence, The Director explains, correlates with high income. It always has. The rich marry the rich in order to preserve fortunes. Before the Industrial Revolution—railroads and steamships and repeating rifles—the rich had as many children as the poor, because no one had reliable birth control, but the infant mortality rate was far lower for the rich. Rich families produced more surviving children than poor families. And smarter children. And these, in turn, married smarter children until the average intelligence of the ruling class was astronomical.

As The Director explains it, the Industrial Revolution took place because every other person in the upper realm of society was a genius. It was a genius bubble.

What impresses Sam most about The Director is how his lips speak. He doesn't make cartoon faces like other adults do when they talk to her. His face has a flat dignity. His face is an oil-painting face. The face of an ancestor, hanging in a museum. He doesn't work his eyebrows or roll his eyes to sell her on anything.

His lips say, "Miss Deel, I am offering you a shortcut to a shortcut to a shortcut to success."

His eyes seem alive, but not. The way a flickering candle or a fireplace makes you feel not totally alone. Standing here is a man who wakes each morning with only one aim: To run the biggest corporation in the world.

Most likely, he speculates, the Renaissance came about due to a similar genius bubble.

Eventually birth control allowed the upper class to have fewer children. Meanwhile better overall health care meant more children of the poor would survive to reproduce. This he calls *dysgenics*. Now, the overall intelligence of humanity was crashing.

To bring about another Industrial Revolution or Renaissance, he explains that Greener Pastures has a plan.

A child's upbringing and genetics decide its intellect. Now parents will be rewarded for giving each child an exceptional education. And every child will see the immediate reward for hitting the books and burning the midnight oil.

As The Director sees it, education will at last achieve the prestige and priority that is its due. By going wide, Greener Pastures will stem the tide of dimwits born to dimwits born to dimwits. People will aspire to bear and raise only valuable children they can auction on an open market. The endgame of Greener Pastures is to bring about the next transformation of civilization.

From Your Practical Guide to Greener Pastures, Eighth Edition, Revised
A Cautionary Tale from Meg and Teri C——
The kid was our first flip. We bought without any caveat emptor. First, we tinkered with his name. No one wants to be ruled by a King Jojo or pray to a Pope Jojo, so we changed it to Jeremiah. Beyond that we slotted him into college-prep courses. Trig, Urdu, the kid was swamped, whatever we tried to hammer into his noggin.

When we emailed his originating family, the email bounced back. Call us slow learners, but the truth was hard to swallow.

We were trying to polish a turd. It was clear that the sellers had tampered with his IQ scores, the nowadays equivalent of turning back the odometer on a used car. Not to sound mean-spirited, but the kid was a lemon.

We'd sunk more than twenty grand cash into Jeremiah, and still had two hundred grand outstanding on the contract through Greener Pastures Finance. When you're that far underwater, what choice do you have? We took him to the local office for GP Finance and explained the situation to the loan officer. We asked to sign a quit-claim deed and surrender Jojo back to his previous holders, but the officer refused. He said they didn't facilitate that type of return, and we'd have to hire a lawyer and take the sellers to court. Just to do that we'd have to hire a detective to locate them. The bastards.

Then we could see this was going to be a whole big megillah.

So we bolted. We asked if Jojo could sit in the office while we went outside to discuss the matter. The kid looked sad but not surprised. The sad reality is that we were probably the third or fourth family to ditch him. And we made a dash for the car, and left little Jojo sitting at the loan officer's desk, and we never looked back.

Full Names Withheld Upon Request

Samantha feels something hidden in her pocket. Something she'd collected as she'd dressed for the funeral. Small and sharp as a razorblade.

They sit in a vast room that holds only two large chairs and a table. Sam has to tamp down the urge to crane her neck and gawk at the paintings on the domed ceiling. A tray on the table holds glasses and bottles, and The Director pours two drinks. He offers one and says, "A toast?"

Sam accepts the glass and caves to her curiosity. She lifts her gaze and takes in the vaulted ceiling, letting the frescoes draw her attention in a slow circle. As she rotates in place, turning her back on The Director, she dips a hand into her jacket pocket and

brings out a shard of glass. It's a blue eye she'd kicked out of a stained-glass face. A busted-out eye of sharp-edged stained glass. And as she marvels over the ceiling, her fingers drop the eye into her drink where it disappears among the blue ice cubes. Turning to face The Director, her free hand says, "Let's trade." She nods. She knows Greener Pastures was watching in Paris. It only follows that she'd be afraid of a possible drink laced with scopolamine. Sam waits a pregnant pause. She nods to indicate their drinks.

The Director doesn't pause, only reaches to take Sam's drink and hands over his own.

Sam accepts the other glass and mimics the way The Director lifts his glass into the air.

The Director says, "Guesswork is dead. Long live Greener Pastures."

They drink a toast.

After they sit, The Director's lips ask, "Tell me what you think you know so far."

Intuition strikes. Sam's hands say what her mind can only guess at. "You cherry-pick. You hunt for kids likely to create seismic shifts in culture and technology, and you weed them out." She waits a synaptic firing or two.

The Director nods. The eye is invisible in his glass.

Sam's hands continue. "You place them in some high-status bureaucratic dead end." She sips her drink. "In effect you warehouse them. They're mothballed until they reach the age when their passion and creativity no longer pose a threat."

The Director lifts a decanter and leans to refill Sam's glass.

According to Mrs. Terry, the mission of Greener Pastures is to preserve the status quo. Those who held power would always hold power. There would never be another Renaissance or Industrial Revolution.

The lips of The Director say, "Such gifted individuals are called *disruptors*."

And if a disruptor declines to be mothballed, he or she is

killed. As humanely as possible. One way or another, they have to winnow out those kids. No more Bill Gates wunderkinds. No more Steve Jobs or Elon Musk boy geniuses. Progress needs some slowing down.

Samantha drinks her glass empty. As if her actions could spur The Director to drink from his own.

Hit Ctrl+Alt+@+Last. The Director drinks deeply. He swallows. He gags. His bulging eyes stare wide, widening, at Samantha as she feigns concern. He's choking. There's something he can't breathe past.

That's when Greener Pastures staff members rush in to save him. Person by person, from the future president of Australia to the future social-media phenom, they try to rescue The Director with the Heimlich maneuver. His mouth bleeds and bleeds, heaving up huge gobbets of blood, vomiting geysers of ketchup. Until it's only the Greener Pastures candidates holding him upright and passing him, ragdoll limp. Until they're only hugging the blood out of him.

Still, they have to try.

At long last, something shoots out his mouth and clatters across the stone floor. A blue-glass eye. A long-lashed eye that conveys incredible love and sorrow.

During all the turmoil, Samantha Deel strolls unnoticed out of The Orphanage and walks through the gardens, and hikes up into the dense tropical jungle beyond.

36

From Your Practical Guide to Greener Pastures, Seventh Edition
A Cautionary Tale from Mindy B——

*I grabbed the knife. Practiced this I had not. We hadn't rehearsed any-
thing because Benjamin, Benny was hopeless. If he so much as sneezed
it sounded fake.*

*The Singers had set out a brisket, sliced and everything nice, with
the carving knife sticking out at a help-yourself angle. Little pots of different World Market mustards sitting around the platter. The perfect
witnesses: the Singers, the Goldblatts, the Futters, the Hartzogs, and the
Taubmans. That girl, that Myra, from the yoga place, she was there for
whatever reason. I waited until Leo Hartzog pointed his camera phone
recording Ilene telling some cockamamie story about pitching something
to Google. That's when I wrapped my fist around the knife handle. Some
stainless-steel German job. A Wüsthof brisket slicer. I'd only downed the
one dirty martini Len Futter had handed me.*

*I yanked the knife out of the brisket. Too hard, obviously. Adrenaline
would do that. Too fast, to judge from how the brisket toppled. Toppled
and rolled, a slab of dead meat batting aside little pots of mustard, ram-
ekins of chopped onions, the brisket escaping the platter and greasing
a path across the limed oak table. From West Elm? From Pottery Barn?
Before taking a plunge—blat—onto poor Yael Singer's cowhide accent
rug. A juicy splat that piqued everyone's attention until I swung the serrated blade toward Benny's neck.*

*I brought the knife down, the dull side, not the honed edge, chopping his
shoulder. With no more force than an Arthurian queen bestowing knight-
hood upon him. All reddish Chinese mustard and yellow-brown honey mustard all over the white collar and sleeve of his Perry Ellis dress shirt.*

His cow-eyed, slaughterhouse expression, here was something my husband could've faked never had he lived to be Methuselah. With my free hand I caught his wrist and twisted that arm behind his back. Held the knife against the bobble of his Adam's apple and sawed it back and forth. Against the little dots of Benny's shaved beard. I held him the way I'd play a hairy cello. No one noticed, what with mustard on the blade, how I was pressing the dull side of the knife against his windpipe, harmless, messy but harmless. Bowing him like a cello. No, no amount of rehearsing could've brought these tears to Benny's eyes or made him keen the way he did. Like a dolphin he sounded, or like some killer whale, keening.

I screamed, "Rape me again, you dirty, penis-stinking bastard, and I'll kill you!" And to Ben's credit he played along with my routine. For his crying, he'd later blame the horseradish. Mixed in some mustard it was, held so close to his tear ducts.

Even in that moment, with the camera phone rolling, I had to wonder who'd served Dylan Thomas those eighteen shots of whiskey at the White Horse Tavern. Wondering: Was whoever poisoned Dylan Thomas someone helpful? Or maybe some bartender who yearned to see dead the preeminent Welsh poet of the age. That's where my head was at: Disassociation. Mine was a classic case of disassociation.

I worked the serrated brisket slicer against my husband's throat with the Goldblatts and the Taubmans watching, and I delivered the line we'd agreed upon. A second time, quietly, almost hissing, "Rape me again, you bastard . . ." This wasn't improvisation. I'd been warning him since Noah's attack. Our performance was all about Noah's attack. And finally Benny recognized his cue.

To his credit, Benny wrapped his strong, sober hand around mine and choked my wrist and rapped my hand, twice, against the Singers' silk wallpaper, until I let go. The knife diving to stab the wood floor at our feet. Chili-infused mustard spattered, red-brown, on the pretty wall.

The scene, like some Old World saying my long-departed Unka would always say at such a time, this was. Half of what the man said a real person knew to not hear, but on occasion my Unka had been touched like genius.

Shock Induction

Yael Singer stooped over the fallen brisket. Her hands hovered above it, hesitated, and sprung forward to clamp together on the slab. Her face twisted in a grimace, she hefted the meat and carried it at arm's length like so much butchered . . . flesh. The awful stain it left, a red puddle, as if Benny had actually bled out. I hadn't been chopping, but they'd seen chopping. Myra from yoga stood with both hands palmed over her mouth. She screamed a moment too late as if meeting some obligation, the silly girl. A thin someone-needed-to-scream scream.

Benny held my wrist with a power I'd forgotten he had. He'd been conflicted about the rape line when we'd discussed it. But I was glad to say it twice. Glad for the camera phone. How it might all look in court. In our moment of faked struggle, I considered collapsing against him, but the mustard would spoil my vintage Bill Blass. I'd had my hair set that afternoon. The look I'd been working was Dynasty. *Like Alexis Colby chopping off Krystle Carrington's head on that one episode of* Dynasty.

"Yael," Benny said when she brought the coats. He regretted the wallpaper, silk handwoven with green parakeets, from China. He'd told her, "The brisket was delicious."

His shirt smelled so good I had to swallow. On the way home, my stomach growling made Benny stop for takeout at Arby's.

With the red-brown smears on his cheeks and nose, Benny looked like our Noah had. Like father, like son. Like Noah had looked coming home from school.

In all honesty my Benjamin, Benny, he wouldn't rape a fly.

Our next act should be me filing a restraining order against him. Subpoenaing hostile witnesses and the like. The first parents to pull this stunt, we were not. Checking into a shelter for abused women, I should be. We needed to build a narrative, I argued, but Benny put the kibosh on my women's sheltering.

Oh, the injustice that my Noah, my baby boy, should be compelled by cold geography to attend the school he did. An institute of higher learning that boasted a Prizon Skillz Track. A verified course of matriculation. A public academy that offered a sex-worker track. A prizefighter my Noah was not. No more than his father could act his way out of a paper bag.

For the steep taxes we paid, our Noah should go to school to be a punching bag?

A boy of such rich talents? Gifted how he was, this boy was wasted on Ansel Park, when where he wanted to go was Delmar Fields, a magnet school. Japanese immersion they had. So what if Delmar Fields was three districts over?

Who the animals were, Noah wouldn't say. Who'd beaten him bloody, they were juveniles. For any lowlife animal boys to see another boy so gifted by fate, these less fortunate would understandably go crazy jealous. Especially seeing how they'd tested too low to amount to anything in life, and Noah, here's Noah excelling in Computer Lab and wanting to take immersion Urdu.

Already families like ours paid for schools, plenty. Paid for the free breakfasts and free hot lunches for such animal vermin who'd send a child home with almost a broken nose. At issue was the principle of the thing.

Driving home from the Singers', I had said as much. "Stop by the Arby's," I'd said. "I want you should see the big picture here."

Mister Social Justice. Mr. Make-Everything-Right, Benny wanted we should foot the bill for private school. Was he crazy? He was crazy. A family should pay twice over, through property taxes and private tuition, for getting their only son not beaten to a pulp?

Benny I told to butt out. Waiting in the drive thru at Arby's, I said, "Don't take this the wrong way, Benjamin, but you are a weak man. A very weak man and a terrible father." I yelled at the speaker for two beef-and-cheese sandwiches. The melty kind. Telling Benny, "No offense."

If I'd managed to hammer anything into Benny's head, it was the fact that he had serious limitations. That he lacked all imagination was chief among them. Our son walks home from school with his eyes beaten purple as two prune Danish, and his nose like a squashed eggplant, and a chipped tooth, his blood all down the front of his shirt, and all this boy's father can say is, "Noah, we'll look into it."

A reaction like that, no father should feel proud of. No, placid Benny could go to his office. Benny could watch the market and type out his buy

and sell orders. Starting with the knife at his throat at the Singers' party and me making accusations of rape, it was I who got the ball rolling. As my boy's only mother, I was planning to rescue him from further assailment.

What would it hurt if I saw my own situation improve? Why couldn't Noah's salvation throw a little good fortune my way? In the car, I checked for napkins in the bag of Arby's. Folded on top the hot sandwiches were paper napkins. "Okay, drive," I told Benny.

I lifted a sandwich from the bag and spread a paper napkin across my Bill Blass. "You only have yourself to blame," I said. I talked while chewing, I was so hungry. "I told you not to wear the Perry Ellis."

It was decided ours would be a marriage in trial separate. What Winchell always called a don't-invite-'em. *With me renting a cheap studio apartment in the vicinity of Delmar Fields, each day I'd leave the house in Ansel Park, sneaking out early so as not to be seen by Yael Singer. Even if I were seen, would it look so bad to be caught apparently still trying to save my marriage with furtive sex? I'd drive Noah to his new school, then spend my day painting in the apartment. Every afternoon I'd dress up in a uniform from a store that sold uniforms, and leave as if to work the night shift somewhere. I'd eat Arby's melty sandwiches every lunch. Day's end, I'd collect our boy and spend the nights at Ansel Park.*

Nights, over the dinner table, Benny would ask, "How's the painting business?"

Noah would be immersed in his Japanese, and I would have a fabled room of my own. That's not to say the Ansel Park house didn't have rooms more than a family of three could use, including the indoor sport court no one ever set foot inside, but a cheap apartment I could move my old college furniture into, my posters and music on compact disc, my paints and easel.

I tried to see the stained grout and splintering cabinet doors the way the future would. The way pilgrims would: As sanctified. Not as shabby, but as a place where a revolutionary artist had set out to conquer the world. I, Mindy B——'s garret. The scuttling brown spot along the base-board, be it a small mouse or a mammoth cockroach, it only added to my street credibility. Future scholars would marvel over this chipped paint.

Lead-based paint. Brain damage waiting to happen. In this neighbor-hood of fetal-alcohol everything.

The edges of asbestos tile peeled up from the cracked concrete floor. To think so many future masterpieces would be painted in the presence of these spiders. That made me think of Charlotte's Web. *And that, those spiders, made me smell the barbeque from the Arby's down the block.*

After a fascinating morning spent applying for social-welfare ben-efits and sketching my fellow applicants, and who should I meet but my next-door neighbor. In the parking lot, he was, the neighbor. Crawling out from under a car. He smelled, but like a soft cheese, like one of the very expensive artisan cheeses, like the free-trade ones packaged afloat in sterile urine sealed within a food-grade pig bladder. Like my Unka always said that I couldn't remember, but that translated to, "A nose is the best judge of character in buying eels."

The stranger popped a beer and handed it to me.

I took a swig. Looked at the can. "I really shouldn't be drinking."

He asked, "Are you expecting a baby?" No male model, his beer belly stretched the front of his T-shirt. Fat he looked, but in that way that made a grown woman feel more feminine. Where the T-shirt rode up in front, his skin showed. Scars were all it was, that skin. Little red train tracks like from staples, like from surgery after being gutted by a landmine. Shiny red train tracks crisscrossing his belly.

I laughed. Took another swig. Shook my hair back. Beer for lunch. I was already blending in.

Dripping plastic faucets and overloaded aluminum wiring that made every light switch feel warm to the touch. I pictured Georgia O'Keeffe in her adobe hut communing with rattlesnakes. Emily Dickinson in her sooty attic isolation.

"So you're not pregnant?" My neighbor wasn't convinced.

I raised the can in a toast. I reached across the space between us, took him around the wrist and twisted until I could see his watch. "Not since . . . ," I noted the time, "two hours ago." His wrist felt solid and hairy. I, Mindy B—, twisted, and he let himself be twisted by scrawny, weak me.

Still, he didn't understand.

"I'm pro-choice, but I didn't get to choose," I stressed. "My old man . . ."
I let my voice trail off in convincing despair.

He looked away as if embarrassed or ashamed on my behalf.

I pressed on. "He didn't want it." I took a long draw on the beer can,
then forced a tragic smile for my fake dead baby.

This would become the pattern of my days: I'd leave Ansel Park each
morning and drop Noah at his new magnet school. A kiln, they offered.
Portuguese immersion. A person could do worse. All that, and Noah had
tested as the smartest from his cohort. While he was in school, I'd pretend
to live at the apartment. Noah, Mister High and Mighty, he wouldn't
show his face at the apartment, he hated the place so much. Chess Club he
took after school, and Rocket Club, to avoid the spiders, and me painting
him. The rent I paid didn't compare to the tuition we saved by fake-living
in the district. Being fake–trial separated. Headed for fake-divorce due
to faked domestic abuse.

I was trying on a new me. This hairy neighbor was the mirror I
watched myself reflected in. I saw the way he must see me. With my French
manicure and waxed legs. Vassar written all over me. I cleared my throat.
"This isn't my real voice."

Maybe he'd buy that I was a glamorous sex worker. Daytime I'd be
at the apartment, winding down. Nighttimes, I implied that I spent my
nights screwing some monied power broker or a captain of industry. This
lie would make the imperfect lie about being a waitress perfect.

Everyone living in the complex, they were a refugee from something.
Somewhere.

His listening was a pit I kept falling into. Or it was a hole I wanted
to fill with my words. I told him I'd contracted gonorrhea in my mouth
one time and had let it go too long, and after that I had this voice, dif-
ferent than before, deeper on account of my vocal cords being scarred.
It was a test. I was shit-testing him. The stranger never looked away or
flinched. Because he was unfazed or because of the language barrier, I
wasn't certain.

Gonorrhea *wasn't likely the first word they taught in ESL so talking*
to him felt nice, relaxed, like talking to a nice dog, like a retired pit bull

you could fantasize having reckless afternoon sex with. The exact words didn't matter.

I looked at his scarred gut. Looked long enough to let him see that I was looking. Someone had tortured this man cruelly and I kept waiting for that cruelty to surface in him.

I remembered Gauguin's bare-breasted Tahitian women. Toulouse-Lautrec's ghastly parlor-house whores. All the women turned into art by men and then forgotten. All the men made famous by discarded women.

Under the sun his pale face had darkened and his dark hair had lightened until they were the same red-brown. A detail maybe no one except a true artist would note. All of those forgotten women I, Mindy B——, would avenge. He would be my muse. Like a Bridges of Madison County*–type situation only with me as the savvy artist and him as the dimwitted foreigner. That seemed like progress as these things went. Trust me, he didn't, not to date. I needed his trust.*

That evening in the car, driving home with Noah, I asked, "Those boys who hit you? How did they hit you?" I added, "I mean, with sticks or what?"

Noah sighed. The only way to describe such a sigh was as a confessional sigh. As if the jig was up. "You ever hear of an outfit called Greener Pastures?" he asked.

I hadn't.

"A kid needs a great education if he wants to net the top bidders," he said.

He told me everything. This Pastures outfit had headhunted him, our Noah, and he could be President of Everywhere if he could get the education.

"Smart kids go to Delmar." Not to mince words, but our Noah had beat himself to his own pulp. That's the genius we'd raised. So to attract the best future possible for himself.

From behind, somebody honked. I hadn't realized I'd slowed to a crawl. To let everyone pass I pulled to the curb. "You did a very good job, with the beating." Nurturing I tried to sound, that's instead of shocked. Then as if just curious, I asked, "How'd you do it?"

Noah's method had been to stand in our indoor sport court and throw a basketball against the concrete wall, close his eyes, and step into its return path. A mouth guard, he wore, like from boxing. God bless him. For smaller bruises he'd catch a racquetball in the face.

When Benny got home and found me with both eyes blackened and a swelling on my forehead so tight it looked to split the skin, that and a fat lip with racquetball bruises on my neck and collarbones, I assured him it was just to keep up appearances. To placate him I brought up how much I'd be getting in food stamps and rent assistance. The government was practically paying us to send Noah to a better school.

On Ivan, the bruises did the trick. His name was Ivan, my neighbor. He accepted my life as a beat-up prostitute brimming with diseases and still kissed my hurt mouth. He seemed to appreciate that I wasn't starved to prison-camp thinness. Not like that Myra from yoga everyone said was so perfect. Ivan would lay claim to big handfuls of me and marvel over my skin. Beautiful I was, merely by not being scarred by barbed wire and dog bites. His smell I got acclimated to, and he wore a fresh condom every time without me having to ask, which put him a notch above Benny on the gentleman scale.

Such a man I'd never met. Ivan wept over my bruises. Kissed them, he did, and swore to end the life of the whoremonger who beat me so savagely. A Fifty Shades of Grey–situation it was, except I had to torture myself. This too seemed like progress as gender relations went.

Noah on the contrary, my genius shaped up to be my problem child. Driving back to the house one night he announced a trepidation about putting the rest of his life up for auction. Such a wishy-washy he sounded like. Taking after his father, I worried. Noah B——, a kid who could be set for life, he wondered if he might be happier being a painter like his mom. Hah! He wanted to paint pictures instead of being the emperor of a communication empire and blessing his parents with millions in Greener Pastures severance fees.

Such a gifted, talented boy he was, Noah wanted to transfer back to Ansel Park. Forget the kiln and Japanese immersion. This, after Ivan had bought me a car, a Ford, so a beat-up prostitute riding the bus I'd

stop having to be. Such a romantic, that Ivan. Driving my clunker Ford back to Ansel Park, I asked Noah, "You want I should tell your father you beat yourself?"

It sounded dirty, but he knew what I meant.

What I didn't say was how relieved I felt. Benny with his always-smiling, Benny B— couldn't hold a candle to Ivan in the sack. But as my Unka was fond of saying, not that I could remember, but in English it came out as, "No delicious eel doesn't get stale."

Noah transferring back to Ansel Park was the out I needed to skate on Ivan.

Not that I told Noah, but I was glad to be fake-reconciling from my fake-separation for fake–spousal abuse. I'd only ever told Ivan my name was Liana. My crap from college, the Ford he'd bought, I could walk away from. Simply leave the keys on the apartment counter and pull the door shut, locked behind me. Ivan wouldn't have a clue where to look. Chapter ended.

Our last afternoon in the sack, I looked around at the mildew. My way to say goodbye was by giving Ivan an Arby's sandwich we could share in a bed I'd never have to make. Dirty sheets I'd leave behind. Disappear I would, step into my Jil Sander slacks and catch the bus to my fake sex workplace. I'd told Ivan the Ford was idling rough, dying at stoplights, so he'd hauled out his toolbox to make repairs. Not the truth, my story, but reason enough to abandon the car. Give it a week, two weeks, and the landlord would show Ivan the unit with my uniforms hanging in the closet, my dirty Arby's bag on the counter while Mindy B— would be vanished Amelia Earhart–style. A fake-murdered sex worker.

Right during sex someone came honk-honking, some car, into the parking lot.

From the window I looked to see Benny pull in. Benjamin, who'd collected Noah from his last day at Delmar Fields. Happy smiling like a dog he was. Like a golden-something dog, he stepped out of his car and called up to my window, "So this is where you live? What a dump!"

Before I could answer, Ivan happened. Tell Benny to run, I wanted to, but Ivan burst out of the apartment door wearing only boxer shorts

and his scars. Ivan snatched up something from his open toolbox beside the fake-broken-down Ford. The whatever tool it was, Ivan ran up and backhanded Benny with it. Swatted Benny across the face. One of those knives it was, like from cutting carpets with a sliding-out razorblade. I could see because Ivan flung the knife away and disappeared sprinting down the street.

Benny, that Benny, he had me going. He truly did, the way he put both hands over his throat and hot Chinese mustard from Williams Sonoma came gushing out between his fingers. But gallons it was, pouring out. Red-brown mustard that must cost a fortune, it was so much, especially for Benny who'd obviously spared no expense to teach me a lesson. Of course, he'd hired this Ivan person, who most likely was mowing someone's lawn in Ansel Park and who wouldn't say no, not if it meant getting paid to screw me and get Benny's revenge for the brisket at the Singers' party. As if this time his throat was really cut, except it looked so fake.

Benny was that kind of petty, he was. All this pettiness just to prove he could act.

From the window I watched my husband sink to his knees. His eyes, he was making the same slaughterhouse eyes he'd made with the brisket knife. Whatever secret apparatus he'd rigged, it was pumping tons, yes, tons of expensive Chinese mustard into the gravel, and he pretended to topple forward. Fake-gasping with Chinese mustard gurgling from both corners of his wide-open mouth. Pretend-twitching, face-down in the gravel, he was, while from the apartment window I filmed with my camera phone and shouted, "Bravo, Benjamin B——!" And, "You're not fooling anyone, mister!"

And like maybe they took acting lessons together, but our Noah jumped out of the car in slow motion and fell, skidded and fell in his hurry, crawling across sharp gravel on his hands and knees he did. Noah crawled to his father to fake a tourniquet around his father's neck using only his bare hands, shouting, "Dad! Don't die, Dad!" even as they're both hamming it up in a flood of Chinese mustard.

Yael Singer, I half expected to jump out from behind a tree, this looked so phony. The Goldblatts and the Futters and that Myra, all watching

to see me get what's coming to me. With sirens, yes, ambulance sirens even my Benny had paid to come screaming closer and closer for added realism. Benny who'd thought of everything, such a stage manager he was. My Benjamin, whom I'd married and given a brilliant son, and who rewarded me by fake-going limp in the arms of our Noah in the dirty parking lot all because of me ruining his favorite Perry Ellis.

A little embarrassed I felt now about how loose I'd got, how soft and loose I'd got so fast with this hired Ivan. That shill, Ivan, I'd wanted him so bad. Well, the joke was on me. Hah-ha! And like something else I couldn't remember, it came to mind. More immigrant wisdom, but when my Unka said it, the words came out, "To a liar the whole world looks like a lie."

Well the joke, the final punch line would be on Benjamin B——, double hah-ha, because he'd never know to laugh. And such a joke! My monthly period I hadn't had in six weeks. It could be more, maybe, but playacting Benny, my playing-dead husband would be raising the child of his hired Ivan.

The scope of his death-scene routine, not to mention the expense, all to humiliate me, Mindy B——. I stood in the apartment window looking down, I did, then put aside filming and started to clap my hands. But very slowly.

Full Name Withheld Upon Request

37

Hark!

What was that? That was pattern int3erruption.

38

Picture Samantha Deel. Sam sits high on a mountainside. Sam strokes her belly. Waiting for the drugs to wear off, but not too fast. Determined to give birth, but not into a world ruled by Greener Pastures. Determined to forever stray off the well-beaten plot.

From a speech given by Esmond Jensen on the first night of the Fiftieth Annual Greener Pastures Alumni Confab
My Fellow Alumni:

What becomes of the dregs? Those kids who test poorly or ingest lead paint? One already sees homeless bands of such children deemed unsuitable to rule corporations or kingdoms. Now that the familial bond is based on market value, won't more children find themselves forced out of the nest by smarter kids bought online?

The children you've seen living in squalor beneath bridges or in condemned buildings are what our industry refers to as Free-Range Candidates. And rest assured they have plenty to offer buyers. Our newest service, named Organ Grinder, will tissue-type dull children and act as an agent to match them with the medically needy who'll pay top dollar for a retina or kidney or the lobe of a viable liver. Blood and bone marrow are big sellers! These payments will allow low academic achievers to acquire the capital needed to bear and raise children they can eventually bring to the marketplace. In the wonderful new economy, no child is unwanted! And no child will be left behind!

Be sure they were grotesque. There were much glare and glitter and piquancy and phantasm. For here capered the world's tycoons and power brokers, the moguls and oligarchs. There were arabesque figures with unsuited limbs and appointments. There were delirious fancies such as the madman fashions. There were much of the beautiful, much of the wanton, much of the *bizarre*, something of the terrible, and not a little of that which might have excited disgust. To and fro in the seven chambers there stalked, in fact, a multitude of dreams. And these—the dreams—writhed in and about, taking hue from the rooms, and causing the wild music of the orchestra to seem as the echo of their steps.

By the second night of the Alumni Confab all the guests are in attendance. All the auctioned children whom Greener Pastures had ever slotted into wealth and power. In the marble halls of The Orphanage they caper as do people who think they're beyond the reach of death. They gambol in the manic frenzy of revelers trying to forget they've sold their souls for these lavish things they never wanted in the first place. With loud music and singing, they drive away the ghosts of each destiny they've refused. Each *idios daemon* they've failed to serve and to liberate.

Throughout the halls and apartments of The Orphanage, the mighty and their attendants go berserk. This is less a celebration than an exorcism, as they hold back the angry genies they've neglected. Those spirits still trapped on Earth because their gift of talents had been rejected. Above this panicked orgy of denial—blasted by music, blurred by alcohol and drugs—the sky explodes in sulfur yellows and acid greens, the fragmented colors of fireworks and neon. Of sky rockets and roman candles.

On the far shore of the murky lake, high on the volcanic slope, Samantha puts her shoulder to a boulder and pushes. Like Sisy-

phus, she grunts with all of her strength, but the boulder doesn't move. Like so many whiz kids, Sam had doubled-down on Trig and ditched Phys Ed.

A grand secret plan is being played out. If only.

A voice in the night says, "Can I help?" A voice she can hear. Her babysitter-slash-bodyguard steps into view. War Dog. He joins her, the two of them straining to free the boulder from its place high on the inside of the dead volcano's lip.

For what could be a moment or a year, they gasp and snort. The boulder gives. It seems only to fall on its side, but then it falls again. It's rolling. The huge rock has escaped its place and crashes onward, leaping, rolling, and leaping through the dark. Unstoppable.

At The Orphanage, the noise of merrymaking masks the loud splash the boulder makes when it hits the lake water.

As Samantha could explain the event, the boulder splashes into the otherwise calm surface of the volcanic lake. It mixes the hot upper layer of water with the frigid layer at the bottom. In that deepest water, the powerful pressure has kept carbon dioxide dissolved. A gas that has collected at the floor of the lake for eons.

Samantha Deel can tell you all about meromictic lakes and trapped CO_2.

About the humane methods used on pigs at slaughterhouses.

As planned, the boulder displaces an amount of that deep water. The water rises toward the surface until the ambient pressure within the lake drops. There the dissolved CO_2 expands, becoming bubbles that combine with bubbles, creating a column of exploding carbon dioxide like the burst of soda from an opened can. In one moment, the lake belches up its entire prehistoric accumulation of CO_2 in a churning blast.

This, Sam Deel would tell you, is how a volcanic lake *turns over*. A cataclysmic limnic eruption. Yes, like an ancient idea.

Exposed to the air, that deep, iron-rich water oxidizes. In an instant, the lake turns bloodred.

Heavier than air, the cloud of carbon dioxide doesn't rise. It spreads like a dense, unseeable fog across the surface of the lake.

By the time this surge of crimson water reaches the steps of The Orphanage, it's hardly a ripple. Hardly warping the reflection of the fireworks and the lighted windows. But behind the wave comes that invisible cloud. A colorless wall of carbon dioxide creeps in on little cat feet.

Apologies to Carl Sandburg.

Hog Butcher for the World . . .

The fog sweeps up the marble steps toward the ranks of uniformed bodyguards and chauffeurs lingering there. They inhale and feel giddy for a giggling moment. They laugh, the goons do, then drop where they stand, and by the time the fog reaches the top step, those people are dead. The fog sweeps through the lobbies and foyers, and drifts along corridors and flutters the curtains in open windows. It flickers candle flames, and tinkles the chandelier crystals. A waiter carrying a silver tray breathes the gas and stumbles and dies still clutching the handles of his tray. And Anne Lewis-Kennedy, who is already in bed in her suite, breathes the fog and dreams glorious rainbow visions before she suffocates.

And while Sam and War Dog watch from the far shore—from the lip of the crater, higher than the heavy fog will ever reach—they hear the blaring music decay. Well, at least War Dog hears it.

A musician blows his last breath through his coronet and slides from his chair to the floor. As does Esmond Jensen, who topples forward onto the keys of his piano and dies in a final jarring chord. The fog fells dancers mid-tango. Among them Noah Brume, still gripping a red rose in his teeth.

Mrs. Terry dies as she has lived, The Red Death, feeling not a thing. And when Myfanwy Mulvaney swims up from the shimmering depths of a marble pool, she will be among the last to die. Wet and confused, she sees the dead bodies heaped around the bar, the dead bodies slumped at tables, still holding their drinks, and

she gasps in shock. Feeling giddy, in a moment she blacks out, slipping below the water, and she drowns.

The fog creeps throughout The Orphanage, sparing no one. Neither dishwashers nor kings.

A parrot escapes to the safe height of a tall tree, where it screeches.

The fireworks stop because the staff in charge of fireworks have all succumbed. And the towers and pavilions of The Orphanage fall so quiet. Then the parrot dies as well.

At that, an utter and profound silence settles over the island.

To break the silents [*sic*] on Honeymoon Island, two birds begin to sing. Very, very high atop the island's tallest tree, a scarlet macaw and a sulfur-crested cockatoo sing the words they've learned from human beings:

> Thick dome of jasmine
> Under the dense canopy where the white jasmine
> Blends with the rose,
> That blends with the rose,
> Bank in bloom, fresh morning,
> On the flowering bank, laughing in the morning,
> Call us together.
> Come, let us drift down together.
> Ah! Let's glide along
> In order for him to be protected by Ganesh
> To the pond where joyfully play
> The snow-winged swans,
> Let us pluck blue lotuses.
> Yes, near the swans with wings of snow,
> And pick blue lotuses.

As Sam and War Dog listen to the birds sing their duet, the latter produces a couple takeout boxes. He passes Sam the *malloreddus alla campidanese* while he digs into the *insalata di polpo*. Such a feast! Such a victory!

Circa 2037, the United States Senate Subcommittee on Education sat down with industry leaders from strategy-based commercial publishing for the stated purpose of stemming the rise in acute ERE poisonings. Hovering over the microphone, an editor from big publishing asked, "Senators, our problem is thus: We have readers diving into *The Lord of the Rings* completely unprepared to battle orcs, and IRL those readers are dying. We have readers confronting Bram Stoker's Count Dracula and IRL dying . . ." Here the editor paused to look at notes spread on the hearing table.

The editor continued, "We have readers immersed in *The Fannie Farmer Cookbook*. Their brain activity suggests they're eating gluttonous amounts of food. But IRL those readers are starving to death, warehoused on hospital wards. Similarly, overseas travel to Paris and the Middle East has fallen to zero, while IRL catatonic and/or comatose patients clutch bootleg, drug-adulterated copies of *The Innocents Abroad* by Mark Twain."

Grumbles of outrage rose in the hearing chambers, grumbles rising to shouts, shouts building to screams. The editor allowed anger to fill the room before taking off a shoe and pounding the shoe against the hearing table. Gaveling for silence.

Once silence reigned, the editor spoke. "With assistance from the DEA, I demand we launch a full-on War on Books! SWAT teams of DEA agents must be dispatched to Edith Wharton's parties and Jay Gatsby's parties, and those MIA readers must be brought safely home."

In closing, the editor said, "It's unfair to label the ERE Program a failure. Only time will tell if our labors have truly borne fruit. Thank you."

Between bites of pasta and sausage, Samantha Deel pitches her voice into the night. "Ah! *Vanitas vanitatum!*" she shouts. "Which of us is happy in this world? Which of us has his desire? Or, having it, is satisfied? Come, children, let us shut up the box and the puppets, for our play is played out!"

At that, something in the dark stirs.

Something bursts from the jungle.

A wild shape comes bounding toward them, something between purse-sized and Marmaduke, with floppy ears and runny eyes and a scar on her rump where the hair never grew back from ringworm as a puppy. Paisley jumps and slurps and licks their smiling faces.

And with *that* our play is played out.

The End.

ACKNOWLEDGMENTS

Author's Note: Upon graduating high school I'd no money for college. To qualify for Pell Grants, I took a gap year during which I worked two jobs: one running copy in a newsroom and the other washing dishes. To keep my head in the education game I read a different library book each week. One week Charles Dickens, the next Edith Wharton. Then Charlotte Brontë and Emily Brontë and Herman Melville and F. Scott Fitzgerald and Lewis Carroll and Leo Tolstoy and Thomas Hardy and Edgar Allan Poe and William Makepeace Thackeray and Mark Twain and Oscar Wilde. If you read this book a second time you'll notice a lot of *Alice in Wonderland* in the drugged aspects and a ton of *Tess of the d'Urbervilles* in the journey of one young woman finding her way in the world. My eternal thanks to those authors who helped me when I had nothing else, during a year when nothing but failure and death loomed. We forget how books can carry us through such times.

Lest they go unsung, my eternal thanks to Anna and Scott and Tim for their support and endless help.

And to Auggie. Welcome to this world, such as it is.

Paramecium.

ABOUT THE TYPE

The body of this text is set in ITC New Baskerville, which was first exhibited by John Baskerville of Birmingham in 1724. Baskerville's development of this new font family signaled a deliberate move away from the Old Style faces that were prevalent in previous centuries. ITC New Baskerville has been revived and updated twice since the dawn of the twentieth century for modern Monotype uses, and it remains a popular choice for setting continuous text due to its simple elegance and inviting legibility.

ABOUT THE AUTHOR

Chuck Palahniuk's fifteen novels include the bestselling *Snuff*, *Rant*, *Haunted*, *Lullaby*, and *Fight Club*, which was made into a film by director David Fincher, as well as *Diary*, *Survivor*, *Invisible Monsters*, and *Choke*, which was made into a film by director Clark Gregg. He is also the author of *Fugitives and Refugees*, a nonfiction profile of Portland, Oregon, and the nonfiction collection *Stranger Than Fiction*. His book of short stories, *Make Something Up*, was a widely banned bestseller. His graphic novel *Fight Club 2* hit #1 on the *New York Times* bestseller list. He's also the author of the graphic novel *Fight Club 3* and the coloring books *Bait* and *Legacy*, as well as the writing guide *Consider This*. His most recent novel, *Not Forever, But For Now*, was a *USA Today* bestseller. He lives in the Pacific Northwest.